# What I Believe

# What I Believe
## a novel

Norma Fox Mazer

HARCOURT, INC.

Orlando   Austin   New York   San Diego   Toronto   London

www.HarcourtBooks.com

Library of Congress Cataloging-in-Publication Data
Mazer, Norma Fox.
What I believe: a novel/Norma Fox Mazer.
p. cm.
Summary: A young girl faces her problems by writing down her thoughts about
the family's personal and financial crises, including the loss of her father's job and
the selling of their home.
[1. Family problems—Fiction.  2. Parent and child—Fiction.
3. Unemployment—Fiction.  4. Moving, Household—Fiction.]  I. Title.
PZ7.M47398Wdc  2005
[Fic]—dc22  2005002252
ISBN-13: 978-0152-01462-9  ISBN-10: 0-15-201462-4

Text set in Brioso Pro
Designed by April Ward

First edition
H G F E D C B A

Printed in the United States of America

For my amazing poet friend, Meg Kearney, whose
belief in me while I was writing this book was
more important than she will ever know.

I also thank my editor, Jeannette Larson, for her quiet
patience and for asking me to write "a few more poems."

*—N. F. M.*

## Memo to Myself

Try not to stumble over chairs or your feet or anyone else's feet.

Do not stare at Casey Ford.

Remember he is the hottest and nastiest boy in school.

Ask yourself why you keep forgetting that.

Remind yourself he told you your front teeth were way big.

Ask yourself why you keep forgetting *that*.

Do not talk about Dad to anyone.

Try to be nicer to Mom.

Try *very hard* to act normal.

## So What Do You Do for Fun, Marnet, Casey Ford Sneered

and I got a bit flustered (he's *so* hot) and stupidly told him about writing in my journal, my notebook, on the palm of my hand, on napkins and scraps of paper, which got me one of those Vicki-Marnet-you-are-strange-strange-*strange* looks, and now I'm thinking if people are gonna look at me like that (and they are, they have, they do, they will), why not just go for it and say although I intend to be a lawyer, writing is *fun* for me, so I write run-on rambling sentences like this one for *fun* and I write crazy things like sestinas and pantoums and all kinds of poetry for *fun*, which I started when I was six and couldn't spell and wrote *Bewaer little gril if you are weerd expeshlee if your daddy has a beerd*, the zingo line being *if you are weerd*, which, even way back then, I knew I was, unlike my big beautiful brothers, who are regular and normal and do regular, normal things like Spencer's sports and Thom's student senate, and that's not all that's normal about them, they also have normal *hair*, which might sound unimportant, but isn't if you have irresponsible, impossible, *ridiculous* hair like mine, which has led to my secret plan, that as soon as I am old enough to do what I want and not freak out Mom and Dad, I will shave it *all off*, and then my strange outside will match my strange inside—in a word, *weerd*.

# Rug Love Sestina

For years, with every fleet beat of my heart,
I loved Revco, each bright brick and stone.
This was where my dad worked, and his eyes
brightened whenever he said, like a song sung
just for me, "Revco is fine, the best. I'll never leave.
Our future is secure, it's one thing I know for sure."

On Take Your Daughter to Work Day, sure-footed,
we raced—his long legs, my short ones—to the heart
of his life, his office. I loved that room, wanted to live
under the desk! On top, photos of us all, silly and stunned
in the sun at our lake house, Mom swimsuited, singing,
Dad building a fire, us kids capering and crazy-eyed.

First time in the office, age six, colored stones
in my pocket, seeing his raspberry rug, I took leave
of my senses, flung myself nose down, closed my eyes
and rolled like a little dog-girl, yipping, "Sure, sure
do love you, ruggy raspberry rug." A rug love song
to please my dad. But, *no.* "Vicki, get up!" I heard.

I stood and saluted, hoping he'd laugh and leave
Discipline Dad on the rug with dog-girl. His eyes
shone on me again. Still, that moment, like a stain,
was hard to clean away. Could even his sure
love be shaken? Scary thought! My heart
took its time slowing. Love is a twisty, tricky songster,

but hate is a twistier, trickier, turnaround song.
*Now* I hate Revco. They fired Dad! "No anger. Leave
it be," he told us. Said he wasn't bitter or heartsick.
"The company had to downsize to save its life. I'll
take my time finding a new job. Hey! This is my shore
leave!" Mom, laughing, picked up one of my stones,

predicted jobs would pelt Dad like rain! The stone
fell. We all scrambled to rescue it for her. Strong
quick Spencer got there first. We cheered, so sure
of our happiness, all of us chattering and lively.
That night, stargazing on the deck with Dad, eyes
on the sky, he pointed out Orion, Betelgeuse. "It's an art

to read the stars, baby." I never wanted to leave
his side—my sure song for so long. Now? His eyes
are stone changed. Just looking at them hurts my heart.

## Doing the Dad Math

1 year, 9 months
336 résumés
897 phone calls
13 flights to 8 states
25 interviews
Zero luck.

## Dad Stats

Height, 6 foot 2
bad he hunches now. His
weight was 180, and 2 times
is a complete circle. He's
56, and half of that is 28 years
he put in at Revco. He used to
sleep 6 hours, times 2 now is
12 every night, plus couch time. He lost
9 pounds, 2 sets of car keys, 3 wallets,
his smile.

# My Brothers

Call me *flatfeet, funny face,*
*Missy Trippy, Vicki Wicky.*
They tease me, squeeze me,
hug me,
shove me.
Love me.

# If I Was a Perfect Person

I would write in this notebook every day, and only beautiful things, and I would give up wanting a dog, which is probably just a bad habit, and I would never be annoyed at Thom for sneezing or wheezing, which is the chief reason we can never have any animals, not even a little wheely-going gerbil, which is just as well because I'd probably get bored with an animal who could only communicate by running in circles, and speaking of animals, which we all are, biologically I mean, if I was even half a perfect person, I would stop thinking that Dad asleep on the couch *again* looks like a zombie, which I guess, to be exact, is not an animal, but not exactly a human being, either, because zombies don't do anything but sleep or go around half dead or, should I say, half alive, like Dad these days, which is a mean, nasty, and really bad thought, especially for a daughter, but it's a thought I think, which I wouldn't think, I'm sure, if I was a perfect person.

# Mom Cinquain

Her skin
smells like lemons
and soap, and when I lean
up against her, I'm a baby
again.

# Bright Red Socks

On field-trip day I wore jeans, a sweatshirt,
woolly red socks, and badly beat-up boots,
which had belonged to my brother Thom.
My darn feet have grown from size five to eight.
Bethani Ollum, smooth-as-syrup girl,
also wore red socks and old hiking boots,
also her brother's. Her motive: coolness.
My motive: cashless. Bethani's clan girls
screamed and oohed and aahed over her boots
and new bright red socks. *So cool . . . I'm going to
ask my brother . . . old boots, oh, beautiful!*
She took my arm. *Girlfriend, we planned it,
didn't we?* Quick as light, the clan began
oohing, *cooing* over my beat-up boots.
That's how I became the new Best School Friend
and Chief Amuser to Bethani O.
It's a toady job—and demanding, too,
but it keeps me busy—and I like that!—
busy enough to blot out, blank out, blink
away—sometimes—what's happening at home.

## Attention, Mommy!
## Your Hair Is Growing Like Grass

Says she can't afford Mr. Willy anymore.
Says she sort of likes having long hair.
Says it's big bucks just to walk through his door.

Says long hair reminds her of being silly and young.
Says she doesn't know where *those* words came from.
Says before she speaks, she should bite her tongue.

Says, how did I get to this point, anyway?
Says, never mind, I'll cut my own hair.
Says, let's not talk about it anymore, *okay?*

# Mrs. Mack, Haralson School Bus Driver, Has Big Fat White Arms

which she leans on the steering wheel while she works
me over. "You're a country-club cupcake, Cookie,
so how come you climb up on this bus
all the time now, and your dad don't drive
you to school no more?"

# triple-time cinquain

mom says
dad should have time
for everything these days,
like fixing the faucet downstairs.
plenty
of time
to write grandpa
—he's alone, hates the phone—
or uncle jud—also alone—
but dad
doesn't
do *anything*—
too tired out all the time.
mom can't even leave him alone,
or won't.

# Announcement, a Tanka

Dad listened, his hands
steepled. Mom did the talking.
"We're putting the house
up for sale. We have no choice.
We're drowning in debt. Drowning!"

# Mom's Monologue

"Listen, kids, I know it's a shock about selling the house. The bottom line is—we've run out of options. We've held on for almost two years, hoping for a break for your dad. You know how hard, how *vigorously*, he's tried to find a job suitable to his experience, but, well, it's not going to happen. I don't want you to repeat this, he's discouraged enough right now, but it's not just the economy. It's his . . . age. *We* don't think he's old, but the marketplace does. It's just horrible, and . . .

"No, forget that, I'm not going there.

"The point is—we can't afford to go on this way. I'm going to be looking for work, but what I can get, after all these years, I don't know!

"But I don't want you guys to worry. I'm just trying to fill you in. We're going to work things out. We'll find an apartment in the city—those twenty miles closer to everything will make a big difference. We'll have one car, not three. And renting means no house taxes, or water and sanitation bills, or paying for garden work and housecleaning, because wherever we live is going to be a lot smaller than this place, trust me on that. And we're all going to pitch in.

"But face it, we're going to have less. Less of everything. Less of everything we don't need. That can be a really good thing. Am I right? Aw, Vicki, don't look at me like that. I know you don't want to move, and we wouldn't if we had any other choice.

"I'm sorry, kids, I'm really sorry . . . but it just has to be. Try to look on the bright side, okay? It's an adventure—for all of us. We're going to be pioneers. Well, not exactly! I just wanted to make you laugh. Come on, you guys, all of you, picture it—less junk in our life, less showiness, everything more down to earth, maybe more like the way I grew up. You'll like that, won't you, Thom?

"Kids, one last thing. I don't want you talking about this to your father. He's got enough on his mind without being reminded of, well, of *anything* . . . I really think this move will help him—help all of us. A fresh start. That has to be good, right?"

# Ten Things I Didn't Say to Mom—and Won't

1. Every time you say, "Don't worry," I worry more.

2. Sometimes I feel like I'm going to throw up.

3. The other day in school, I was so nauseous I had to go to the nurse's office. She asked if there was any tension at home.

4. I said no.

5. You and Dad made the decision to sell the house. You didn't ask me or Spencer or Thom anything, but it's our life, too. It's *my* life. My life right here on Sweet Road, where I've always been. Where I belong.

6. I never thought about *my life* before.

7. I didn't have to. I just lived it.

8. I will never just stay home and take care of my kids, like you—if I even have kids.

9. I'm going to go to law school, and I'm going to work and have a career and never be poor again.

10. And, P.S. I don't want to be a pioneer.

# The Real Estate Agent

"You must be Vicki, right? I'm Nina Byrd.
I guess you've heard from your mom about me."
Lemon hair, lemon dress, she warbles a laugh, golden.

"This house is great, it'll show really well.
I told your mom, it's going to sell in no time."
She holds a sign, HOUSE FOR SALE, bright letters, red.

"Okay, Vicki, will you give me a hand here?
Should we land this baby right over there?"
She pushes the sign into grass, green.

"Don't talk much, do you? Excited to be moving?
I'm sure delighted to be selling this house."
She's hammering, bracelets clinking, silver.

"Well, this is part of the job I don't fancy.
Say, Vicki, you want a chance at this?"
Two-handed, I squeeze the hammer, blue.

I punch and pound that sign
Deep into the ground, but not deep enough.
Not far enough to bury it, bury it, black.

# We're Still Here on 5555 Sweet Road

but strangers peer in rooms, run water
in sinks, open all doors, tap walls,
ask us, How old is this house?
Ever have any problems?
Does the skylight leak?
Is the school safe?
Cellar dry?
And by
the way, why
are you moving?
Is something wrong here?
There must be a reason.
Is it neighbors—do they fight?
What about taxes—out of sight?
It's such a nice house, why would you leave?
Why?

# Lies in the Locker Room

I pulled on my jeans and lied to Bethani that selling our house
and moving to the city was just a goofy idea that my parents
came up with for no reason at all, and putting on my socks
I lied that they were *like that,* which I said rolling my eyes
as if they were sort of crazy and impulsive,
then buttoning my shirt, I lied that they probably wouldn't
go through with it, and while I pulled my hair into a ponytail
I lied that even if they did
I didn't care
no I didn't
not one
little
bit.

# Subj: Moving Plans? Really?

Date: June 15  Time: 5:35 P.M.
From: Ms. Ainsworth  To: Victory Marnet

Ciao, Vicki! It's Friday night, and I missed catching you for a talk this afternoon. I hear through the grapevine that you might not be coming back to Haralson Country Day School in the fall. That is sad news! I will miss you. You're one of my best language arts students, not afraid to experiment. But are you working on those sestinas and pantoums we talked about? I'm so proud of you for tackling those poetic forms. Have you tried a villanelle yet?

Is there anything I should know about your move? Do we need to schedule a little meeting for you to talk about anything? Do you need to vent? I get the feeling that you might be a tad troubled.

See you on Monday, and remember I'm always here for you.

Your Team One language arts teacher,
Ariel Ainsworth

Subj: Re: Moving Plans? Really?
Date: June 15   Time: 6:20 P.M.
From: Vicki Marnet   To: Ms. Ainsworth

Ciao, Ms. Ainsworth! Yes, my family is planning 2 move. Our house is up 4 sale. Thank you 4 asking, but nothing is wrong. Anyway, nothing I need to talk about.

CU SOON,
Vicki Marnet

P.S. Yes, I've been fooling around with sestinas and pantoums, and like you said, it's a kind of puzzle, fitting all the pieces together. I think it's good practice for thinking logically, which I'll have to do when I'm a lawyer. Thanks for showing me!

P.S. again: I know we've talked about this before, but just to remind you, we don't have to tell anyone else about the poetry stuff. Okay? Big thanks!

## sold for cash

mom's grand piano and the white down couch
dad's red sports car with leather seats
thom's telescope (but not his microscope)
spencer's snowmobile and alpine skis
my comic book collection

*you got off easy*
spencer said.
thom agreed.

## News

The Cameron family is buying our house.
The Cameron family has two boys and a girl.
The Cameron kids will go to our school.

## Anti-News

I don't want that Cameron girl in my school.
I don't want that Cameron girl in my house.
I don't want that Cameron girl in my room.

## No News

is said to be good news—
now I see
why.

## Sweet Road Rap

Don't wanna leave you, gonna grieve you.
Feel like crying, but trying not to, not to
B 2 blue, 'cause I know the wrangle tangle
of Mom who's kinda mad & Dad who's 2 sad,
& Spence & Thom & me, guess we're the way
we have 2 B: Spence teasing, Thom wheezing,
me tryin' 2 B pleasing.
Whole family freezing.
Ya C?

# What Mom Said While Tagging Stuff for Sale

3 TVs

"How many do we need?"

8 sheet sets

"Someone else will like these."

25 crystal wineglasses

"They'd probably just get broken when we move."

3 digital cameras

"When's the last time anyone took pictures?"

1 teak dining room table

"This is way too big for an average apartment."

15 towels

"You'd think we set records for cleanliness!"

1 fur coat

"Nobody wears fur anymore, and I approve."

1 small red velvet couch

"Vicki, oh! You used to take your naps on this."

# Overheard at the Tag Sale

"I know how these rich
        people are. They put out all
            their garbage, their old
                leftovers, trashy stuff, junk,
                    and then they want big prices."

## Scary City Thoughts
## after Listening to Bethani

Everyone knows the city
is deadly, dangerous, dirty
most of the kids have guns
half of the kids are out of control
and the other half are on the skids
IQs are lower, morals are shiftier
people are meaner and slower.

Everyone, everywhere, knows—it's common knowledge
everyone in the city is scared
of everyone else—and no one goes to college
and no one moves to the city willingly
and everyone wants to get out
*just get out.*

Everyone, everywhere, knows this
everyone except my parents.
We're going in.

# Mrs. Mack Pretty-Talks Me after School

smiling, showing her brown teeth, saying, "You take care of
yourself, Cookie. See you, little darlin'," as if she loves me, as if
we're buddies, but her eyes are saying something else, her eyes
are saying, *You're a pity puppy now, poor people now, not so high-
and-mighty now.* I pass her back a smile, give a jaunty swing to
my knapsack, like *Who cares what you know,* but that traitor
sackful of books slams my leg, as if it's telling me, *You care,
Cookie!* My leg stings and I stumble down the bus steps, but
I keep holding on to my smile and, on impulse, sassily (oh,
stupidly!) wiggle my butt, which gets me nothing but a catcall
from Casey Ford, who always seems to be around when I make
a fool of myself, and it's only now, hours later, that I see the
black-and-blue bruise stretched across my calf and shaped
almost like a house. I guess it's a souvenir of Sweet Road.

# Weather Report

Mom, cloudy.

Dad, overcast.

Spencer, sunny all day.

Thom, possible storm brewing.

Me, unsettled conditions.

# Memo to Myself

Do not hate the Cameron people.

Try to remember it's not their fault.

Do not get mad at Mom.

She can't help talking about the apartment she found.

Do not get mad at your brothers.

They can't help talking about their new school.

Do not get mad at Dad.

He can't help not talking about anything.

# On Moving Day I'm a Robot

helping to pull apart my bed, take down my curtains, carry
chairs, lamps, and boxes out to the U-Haul, robotically passing
everything up the ramp to Dad, trying to laugh at Spencer's
jokes, trying not to cry because we're leaving the house where
I've always lived, and hours pass, the rooms are nearly bare,
voices echo from upstairs to down, and in the empty kitchen
I pick up the last chair and bash it on the floor, bash it, bash it,
*bash it,* and then I am crying, and all the rooms are crying, and
the windows are like big bare sad faces, and I want to bawl at my
family, *We're leaving our house, we should do something special, we
should say a prayer,* so I do, I pray with my face against the wall,
and then somehow time has passed again, and Dad and my
brothers are in the U-Haul, and Mom and I are in the car
behind them, and we're rolling slowly down Sweet Road when
Spencer sticks his head out the window and yells something,
and Mom asks, *What did your brother say?* and I say I don't know,
but to myself I think he must have been crying out, *Good-bye,
house . . . good-bye, Sweet Road . . . good-bye, good-bye . . .*

# Dialogue in the Car with Mom as We Pass the Welcome-to-Winslow Town Sign, and She Lights a Cigarette

*Vicki:* Mom, what are you doing? You're smoking! When did you start smoking?

*Mom:* Yes, I am smoking, and don't tell me I shouldn't. I know that. It's just for now, in the present circumstances.

*Vicki:* When did you start?

*Mom:* Oh, years ago! I smoked in college. I gave it up when I met your father. He told me it made my breath stink and my hands smell. Quote, unquote.

*Vicki:* I mean, now. When *now* did you start?

*Mom:* I don't know, Vicki! I just did. A few weeks ago—or maybe months, I'm not sure. What does it matter? I'm going to stop, don't worry.

*Vicki:* When?

*Mom:* And don't do what I'm doing. You know I've told you about the dangers of smoking. I don't take back any of that. There's nothing good about it, nothing.

*Vicki:* Right. When?

*Mom:* When what?

*Vicki:* You'll stop *when*. Vicki said patiently.

*Mom:* I'll stop when things calm down.

*Vicki:* When will that be? Vicki said reasonably.

**Mom:** How do I know when things will calm down? I'm not a fortune-teller! Soon, I hope. And why are you commenting on yourself like that?

**Vicki:** I just like to. Vicki said thoughtfully.

**Mom:** Sweetie, please. City traffic makes me nervous, and you're really not helping. And don't say anything to your father about my smoking, he doesn't know, and I won't be smoking in the house.

**Vicki:** We don't have a house anymore. It's an apartment. Isn't it an apartment? That's what you said, it's an apartment.

**Mom:** Vicki, sometimes you are the sweetest girl in the world and sometimes you make me want to tear out my hair! When did you learn to be so annoying? You're right, it's an apartment. Must you say it as if it's a bad word? Lots of people live in apartments. Most of the world lives in apartments, probably.

**Vicki:** Mom, you don't know that.

**Mom:** I said probably, didn't I? I lived in an apartment when I was growing up. Oh, this is it! Look! Look at the street sign. Second Street. That's our street. Check the numbers on the houses. We're 22 Second Street. Don't you think it's lucky, all those twos?

**Vicki:** Mom, I don't think luck has anything to do with it. There's a lot of traffic on this street, isn't there? Ouch! And *potholes*! Jeez, they should fix this street!

**Mom:** Vicki said helpfully.

## the landlady, mrs. dann

old blue jeans
frilly blouse
white curly hair
yellow teeth
brown marble eyes

## a white bulldog

sits in the window
on the third floor
hoarse-voiced
barking
at us

# mrs. dann speaks

here's your key, you better make copies.
where's all your things, still on the way?
everything's clean, you don't have to worry about that.
up there on the third floor is my other tenant.
mr. marty and his mr. rose been with me many years.
they don't give me trouble, no, they never do.
that's the way i like it, you'll be the same.
they wanted the second floor, but i said no.
i didn't want any dog toenails clickety-clickety-clacking
over my head, you see what i'm saying?
but you people are good people, i can tell
you won't mind.

# Eating Chinese Takeout on Our First Night

Precariously perched on a pile of boxes,
Spencer's plugged into his music,
head nodding, fingers drumming, not noticing me
cross-legged on a pillow, writing this on a paper plate.
Dad, eyes closed, rolls an empty rice carton between his palms
as if it's a crystal ball telling him something none of us know.
Mom's rubbing her hands as if she's freezing.
She stretches out her foot and nudges Thom,
who's lying on the floor, reading, coughing, and wheezing.

*Son,* Mom says, *get off the floor, in a minute you'll be sneezing.*
*This whole place needs cleaning, but it's got character.*
*Don't you agree, Larry?*
Dad keeps rolling the rice carton.
*Larry, are you okay, please stop doing that,*
*it's getting on my nerves, and does anyone want*
*more sweet*
*and sour?*

# Memo to Myself on Entering MLK School

Watch what's going on, but don't be obvious about it.

Head up when you're walking in the halls.

Try really hard not to stumble over *anything*.

Smile, but not so big that you feature your front teeth.

Figure out who's *down,* but do not suck *up.*

Check out the clothes and dress accordingly.

Remember, these are cool city kids.

## Being a School Newbie

is something like
being a newborn
only not adorable
to anyone
this time.

## How It Is at Home after One Week

The TV lives in the kitchen, chairs crouch on the couch,
and boxes bang around the hall. Finding a clean towel is a
big deal, and no one knows where the toothpaste is hiding.
Glasses are still stuffed with crunched-up, nasty newspaper,
the toaster oven hates us, and sticky packing popcorn pops
up everywhere. Yesterday, those white nasties slip-tripped
Mom, who fell down on her knees and cried. I cried, too.

# Answering Machine Duet

*Hey there. It's Bethani here. Uh-huh, this is my personal private
phone, so leave me a message after the tone. Don't bore me, pul-ease.
Make your message fun, and you'll be number one on my callback list!*
Hi, Bethani! I thought you might like to hear from me. I started
in my new school. Uh, well, zo zorry I have nothing really funny
to zay today. I'll be thinking about it for the next time, though.
Wazzup, anyway? Call me!

*Hey there. It's Bethani here. Uh-huh, this is my personal private
phone, so leave me a message after the tone. Don't bore me, pul-ease.
Make your message fun, and you'll be number one on my callback list!*
Hello, hello, hay-lo again. It's Vicki. Well, life is sort of interesting
here. Or different, anyway, if you know what I mean. Remember
those things you said about guns and kids in the city and stuff?
Whew, baby! I haven't forgotten. I'm watching my back, I'm
telling you! No close calls *yet* in MLK Middle, and that is not
Milk Middle. Anyway, hope to hear from you soon, if not even
sooner. Call me!

*Hey there. It's Bethani here. Uh-huh, this is my personal private
phone, so leave me a message after the tone. Don't bore me, pul-ease.
Make your message fun, and you'll be number one on my callback list!*
Bethani, is your answering machine not feeling well? A tad sick?

Has a virus? I've been leaving you messages—uh-huh, *several*. Sooo, topic of the day will be—home base. My home-base teacher, Mr. Franklin, is African American—he has us all for language arts, too. He wears wire-rimmed glasses and his hair in a long ponytail. I don't know what I think of him yet. Oh, in case you're baffled, home base is what they call the team room here. It's all sort of different, including the teachers and the kids. Lots of black kids, lots of brown kids, lots of Asian kids, plenty of white kids, too. None of them too friendly. Anyway, no guns, at least—tell you more when you call.

*Hey there. It's Bethani here. Uh-huh, this is my personal private phone, so leave me a message after the tone. Don't bore me, pul-ease. Make your message fun, and you'll be number one on my callback list!* Bethani? Are you there? Hello? Hello? Oh, well . . . good-bye.

# I'm Calling Bethani Ollum Way Too Often

It's so tempting—like almost stepping off a cliff—
how close to the edge can you go and still not fall?
I called four times this week—four times too many!
Saturday she answered. I started talking fast,
lunging right off that cliff into a reckless riff
on school, kids, teachers, my misery, misery,
misery, missing *nothing.* Top-speed tongue tripping.
Barely curbing the impulse to bleat, *No one talks*
*to me. I eat alone. I wish I was back home.*
Sniffing like a cat, she switched the subject fast.
I don't blame her. I let my mouth run—*no playing*
*field, no art or music, no fast-track classes. None.*
Mom says most of the time you get what you ask for.
I guess I was asking for Bethani Ollum
to feel sorry for me. She obliged! Gulped out
my name gleefully. *Poor, poor, poor little Vicki.*
Those words—her voice—they painted a sorry picture
of me—a poor, pathetic, pitiful creature.
I'm going to learn to speak less and, I *vow,*
I *promise,* from now on I'll think first, not just fast.

## A Very Long Sentence About Two Very Short Neighbors

This morning, looking out my window, I saw Mr. Rose, who was wearing a blue and red striped scarf and a gray porkpie hat, and Mr. Marty, who was also wearing a blue and red striped scarf (on which he was drooling big white doggy drools) walking slowly up and slowly down the driveway, then slowly up and slowly down again, which looked so boring it made me feel sorry for them both (but mostly for Mr. Marty), so I stuck my head out the window and called in a cheery voice, "Mr. Marty and Mr. Rose, hello, good morning," but neither one looked up, and Mr. Marty didn't give me even a short friendly bark, which was kind of crushing, but I reminded myself that they're both not only short and stumpy, but on the old side and maybe even a little deaf, so this afternoon when I came home from school and saw the two of them walking up and down the driveway again, I waved and called and waited, but Mr. Rose didn't even glance my way and neither did Mr. Marty, and now my feelings were getting hurt, but I reminded myself what my brother Spencer likes to say, *There's always tomorrow to try again*—so I will.

# Daily News Brief

Mom chewing on a pencil, checking sales.
Dad, talking low, on the phone.
Thom reading, wheezing, pushing at his glasses.
Spencer shooting hoops outside, alone.
Vicki watching, writing this poem.

# The Landlady Stops Me for a Little Chat

**Mrs. Dann:** There you are, Vicki. Aren't you a little late getting home?

**Vicki:** (*Aren't you a little snoopy?*) Oh, no, Mrs. Dann. I just took my time.

**Mrs. Dann:** Have you made a lot of friends in your new school?

**Vicki:** (*Dozens. Hundreds. Thousands.*) Well, uh . . . mmm . . . sort of . . .

**Mrs. Dann:** No one's home upstairs. Your mother's at work.

**Vicki:** (*Thank you so much for the news flash.*) Yes, I know she is. Her new job.

**Mrs. Dann:** Some folks would turn up their nose at answering a phone in an office, but your mother has a good attitude. No la-di-da there. Now, your quiet father has to find something. He's out there looking today. I hear that your brother Spencer is an excellent athlete and has joined the cross-country team. And the other one, Tim—

**Vicki:** Thom.

**Mrs. Dann:** —is very smart and a top chess player. Busy boys, but shouldn't they be spending more time looking after you, instead of leaving you alone every afternoon? What do you do upstairs all alone? Sometimes it sounds like you're jumping.

**Vicki:** (*Sometimes I am!*) I wash the breakfast dishes, set the table for supper, do some homework. Mrs. Dann, I have to go now.

**Mrs. Dann:** Now, don't run up those stairs, you hear me, an accident could happen. Wait, you didn't take your mail. Here you are, mostly junk mail. Isn't that lucky!

# Unrequited Love Poem

He doesn't know I exist
but I'm in love
with that too-fat
low-slung
waddly
drooly
dirty
white
dog,
Mr. Marty.

# Ten Questions to the Universe

1. Why is Sara Madison, who sits next to me in home base, the girl I most want to know?
2. Why do I write poetry?
3. Will Thom and Spencer get to go to college?
4. Will I?
5. Could I tell Thom and not Spencer that I write poetry?
6. Could I tell Mom and not Dad?
7. Why do I keep thinking about us being poor?
8. Why don't I remember there are lots of people who don't even have homes?
9. Why do I keep remembering my pathetic phone calls to Bethani?
10. Why do I obsess over phone calls when Dad still has no job, and Mom spends every evening trying to figure out how much we still owe people, and my brothers are making friends and I'm still not, and I should be thinking of what to say to Mr. Franklin about why I'm not buying even one book through the book club, although, as he pointed out, it's no more money than a meal at Big Burger, which, as he also pointed out, is a place where most every one of us leaves plenty of change, and why didn't I have the guts to say to him, *Not me*?

# at the end of the day

mom throws off her jacket, kicks off her shoes,
hisses, soft as a shiver, *don't anyone dare*
*talk to me for at least ten minutes.*

dad leans on his elbows, chin in hands.
he's forgotten to shave—*again.* that look
is cute on pretty boys in the ads.

my brothers suck up supper,
sitting on the edge of their chairs,
then streak out, shouting *gotta go, good-bye!*

i do homework and i do sleep
to a second street city lullaby—
sirens, horns, tires screeching, sometimes a scream,
sometimes people singing.

# What I Miss

Curling up on the couch with a book I *bought*
*Always* having money in my pocket
Not *ever* worrying about money
Mom cooking good stuff *every night*
Hearing *chickadees,* not pigeons, in the morning
*Clean* sidewalks, lots of locker space
Playing hockey, swimming in the *school* pool
Dad saying, *I'll take care of it, no problem-o,*
*everything will be fine.*

# I Mostly Like Mr. Franklin
# but I Find Myself Trying to Avoid His Eyes

which seem to see everything, so this morning in home base, after he announced, "Ladies and gentlemen, last call for book-club orders," and then beckoned me up to his desk, it made me jumpy, and I walked very slowly up the aisle, looking back, and I saw Sara Madison watching me, which made me jumpier, and then Mr. Franklin said, "Get a move on, Vicki," which made me even jumpier, so when he said, "No books for you, Vicki? Any problem?" (and I knew he meant money), whatever *it* is that makes me do things impulsively, *it* was urging me to tell him the truth, to go ahead, spill it—*you don't have money and you can't ask your mother and it's not his business and he has to stop asking you questions!*—and I would have said it—the words were right there on my tongue, pushing to get out—and regretted it, *of course,* but the bell rang, and I was saved. Saved by the bell. I am sometimes a lucky girl.

## Money Tanka

In the cool morning
I am alone in the house
searching through jackets,
coats, and shirts, looking for change,
glad that no one can see me.

# What I Wish

I wish that certain boys roaming the halls wouldn't stare at me
and sometimes howl for reasons I don't want to know.
I wish there was a good reason that some girls have beautiful chests
and mine is as flat as my belly is round.
I wish I had a friend to be jokey with
and that my mother would make a joke now and then
and give up always being so serious.
I seriously wish that boys wouldn't hold their girls around the neck
as if they were going to choke them
and that girls wouldn't let boys hold them around the neck
as if they're ready to be choked.
I wish that exercise took more brains than patience,
that I didn't hate cornflakes, which make an easy breakfast,
that I was less flakey about cooking,
and that all the skinny girls
who look like they have no appetite didn't blue me out.
I wish that Dad would get cured of his blues
and I wish that wasn't too much
to wish for.

# If I Was a Perfect Person

I wouldn't write *was*, I'd write *were* and the spirit of Ms.
Ainsworth would rejoice, but more than that, *I'd* be rejoicing
today and *my* spirit would be happy today because Dad has
a job, *at last,* and I *am* happy and I *do* rejoice, but not totally
because Dad's eyes are still half closed, and because he said, as if
it was a joke, "A night watchman is a job that a barking dog can
do even better than a man," and I laughed too hard, so glad to
hear him make even a lame joke, but it's true that being a night
watchman is *way, hugely* different from being an executive with
his own office and his own assistant and his own big desk and
raspberry rug and pictures of us on the big desk, and in fact
you might say it's not just *different,* but an enormous, colossal,
gigantic *comedown,* and isn't this what we're all secretly thinking,
and aren't we all pretending, playing the game of the-Marnets-
are-just-an-ordinary-little-family-unit-getting-over-a-few-
ordinary-little-bumps-in-the-road-of-life, which you could say
is just being kind to Dad *or* you could say we're a bunch of
hypocrites, acting one way, thinking another, *or* you could say I
am a sarcastic, spiteful, snotty person to even think such a thing
about my family, and if that's true it explains why I still haven't
made any real friends at school, which I surely would have, if
I was even half of a half of a perfect person.

# Report Carding Myself

Social skills. D minus
Class participation. D minus
Making friends. F
Keeping promises to self. D

Close to failing on all fronts.
Recommend
intervention
suspension
detention.

# My Brothers Give Me Advice

**Spencer:** First thing, stop even *thinking* about Bethani Ollum. She may be cool in your old school, but she's a loser in life. The kids at MLK are cliquey, you say? Suck it up. No use having a fit. You're tougher than that! What's that old thing Dad used to say—go with the flow? Yeah, that's it.

**Thom:** Spencer's right—the present is what counts—the *now,* the moment, real time. Read any of the great spiritual teachers and that's what they tell you. The time is now, not the past, not the future. *Now* is where you are. *Now* is real. *Now* is what you have to focus on. Look around, find someone else alone, or maybe just someone looking your way. Reach out to that individual, okay? You do that sincerely, and guaranteed, you can't miss.

## Memo to Myself
## after Listening to My Brothers

Call Bethani one more time—to kiss her off.

Don't be thinking all the time *if only . . . what if . . . when . . .*

Focus on the present, the *now* moment.

Smile at people you recognize—even if you have to paste it on.

Pretend you don't mind that you're mostly still eating alone.

Remember, no one else knows you're scared and sad.

# Blue Bic Pen Pantoum

I did it, at last—reached out and took a different path.
Sara Madison was shaking her blue Bic pen, wrist flying.
We sit next to each other in history, home base, and math.
"Violent, girlie," I said. "Is that thing dead—or dying?"

Sara was shaking her blue Bic pen, wrist flying.
I dug out my courage and tapped her on the arm.
"Whew, violent. Is that thing dead or dying?"
Sara snickered. "Dead, sister. Can't do it any more harm."

I found my courage, leaned over and tapped her arm.
We'd talked, but joking around was definitely new.
Sara was cute! "Dead, sister. Can't do it any more harm."
I tossed her my pen. "This one's alive. Sorry it's not blue."

We'd talked before, but this joking was definitely new.
I had Sara down pat in my mind for a white-girl snot.
I tossed her my pen. "This one's alive. Sorry it's not blue."
Reaching out, like Thom said, but not expecting a lot.

I had Sara down in my mind as a white-girl snot—
the way she held her head, her chin tipped in the air!
But I reached out, only not expecting a lot,
unsure about her, plus stupidly worried about—*my hair?*

The way Sara held herself, chin tipped in the air,
threw me off. I joked about a "pen funeral," but
being unsure about her and all worried about my hair,
I stumbled around, then wished I could just cut

out my tongue. Actually, I was sort of funny, but
Sara just looked at me deadpan, almost cross-eyed.
Great! I goof up my joke, wish I could cut
out my tongue, then blurt, "Jeez, I'm totally fried."

And she looks at me deadpan, nearly cross-eyed,
sending the message that she thinks I'm strange.
Terrific! I'm humble, saying I'm totally fried,
making excuses for being me—as if I could change,

if I only tried! *Not.* Yeah right, girlie, I *am* strange.
Then I heard her say, "Wanna eat lunch with me?"
I zoned back in, dug in my pocket, rattled change—
two dimes! "Is this a date?" I shot back. "I *might* be free."

Oh, yes, I heard her say, "Eat lunch with me?"
Today I reached out and took a different path,
played it funny and droned, "I *might* be free."
I sit next to Sara in history, home base, and math.

# Walking to Lunch with Sara Madison

she turns her big green searchlight eyes on me.
"Vicki, what things do you like to do best?"
I am not about to confess to her,
*I write poetry, make up funny rhymes,*
*noodle around, try new stuff all the time.*
I hold my hands a span apart, then close
with a clap and bridge her searching silence
with, "How 'bout you? What do you like to do?"

"Oh, me!" Sara says, as we stand in line,
"I'm easy. I'm totally in love with
acting. Big, *big,* love! I watch videos
almost every night. Like my dad told me,
I'm studying how the great ones do it.
Acting genes must run in my family.
My mom was a model when she was young.
My little sister sings Beyoncé songs
every other minute—so annoying!
My dad—he's an oldies radio buff,
he does sound effects, does them all—honks, barks,
quacks, footfalls—you've gotta hear him sometime,
Vicki, it's a riot! He has a show
of his own here, too. It's on every day—

Mike Madison's Mic, ninety-one point five
on the AM dial, at five A.M."

"Five A.M.?" I say, taking my tray. "Whew!
But I will listen for sure some morning.
Wow, your father is on the radio.
That's awesome, Sara. It's so impressive."
Sara's smile signals *satisfaction,* and
she squeezes my arm hard. "'V., I'm so glad
that we're friends now. Are you, too?" I nod, smile,
wondering what stories I'll tell, what words
I'll find to say when Sara wants to know
what work, what job, what talent
my dad has.

# Shopping with Mom in the Supermarket on Saturday

No, we can't afford it.
Put back two of those.
We can get along without that.
Well, I'm sorry, maybe next week.
Get the economy size.
We'll buy that when it's on sale.
Uh-uh, we're not buying steak.
No, no lamb chops,
blood oranges,
lychee nuts,
chocolate,
candy,
cake,
soda.
Sorry.

# Sara Stuns Me with Three Questions

starting when we're walking out of school together and all of a sudden, she comes out with, "So what made you stop being such a snob?" and before I can even squawk, *Me, a snob?* she surges on, "Before the other day, you never once looked my way," lobbing that ball into my court so coolly, I can almost see her bouncing on her toes and twirling a tennis racquet, which instantly sends me the picture of Dad at the country club before we had to sell our membership, twirling his racquet and talking tough tennis tactics to me—*Baby girl, go for every shot, never let down, it's preparation for the rest of your life*—and me nodding solemnly to please him, but secretly, sublimely sure that I didn't ever have to think about *the rest of my life* or *preparation* or any of that stuff Dad was always talking about, but now I see that I am *in* the rest of my life, and at this moment in my life I want to lob that snob ball back into Sara's court and make her run to answer it, but I've been taken by surprise, my brain is stopped, stripped of answers, so the Snob Question hurtles past, and I only manage a feeble return, "Hey, I'm new here, seems like you should have been the one to—" but Sara's voice jumps right over mine, like jumping over the net, with "Whoa, sister! It never occurred to you that I'm new this year, too?" and that's stunner question number two, and no, it never did occur to me and now, how do

I change the air between us, filter it back to laughing about dead pens and such, but even as these thoughts thud through my mind, my mouth is saying, "So if you're new, then you know it's hard work being a newbie, everyone here sticks so tight with their own posse, like the black girls ignore us totally, 'cause we're white, but the white girls aren't any better—" but Sara's jumping the net again with, "What makes you think I'm white? I'm biracial. My dad is African American," and she crosses her arms and turns her searchlight eyes full blast on me, as if asking, *So now what excuse do you have?* and for this one, a fourth, but unuttered question, I have an answer at last—*No excuse. None!*— but I don't say it, because Sara is still giving me the long, deep, challenging look, which I feel obliged to give back, which I know is stupid, but I'm reasoning that I can't lie down and play dead-girl, gotta give as good as I get, which is even more stupid, because that's how wars start, and I'm not a warrior, in fact I'm probably a pacifist, so while we stand there, semiglaring at each other, I dig a stick of gum out of my pocket and hold it out as a peace offering to Sara, who says in a prissy voice, "I never chew a whole stick of gum. My mother says it looks gross, and I agree," so I snap the gum in half, give her half, and we pop the gum into our mouths at the same moment and begin chewing, and right then, with Sara's smoldery gaze simmering down, I have an almost irresistible impulse to make a pun about *almost gumming up our sticky friendship*, but I decide not to push my luck and just chew harder.

# At the North Light Mall with Sara

There's *stuff* everywhere, and I want all of it. I want everything
I see—socks, scarves, earrings, purses, T-shirts, even fake flowers,
which I've never liked, but right then, cruising with Sara from
one shop to the next, there's nothing that I wouldn't buy. It's
been so long since I've had anything new, and I'm as dizzy as
the time I sneaked a glass of wine when I was not quite nine.

Passing the bike shop, I want a mountain bike, even though
there are no mountains here, and in the record shop, I want
the new Spike Sunders CD, even though I don't like his music.
If I had money, I'd buy shoes with those skinny little heels, even
though I couldn't get my feet into them, and I'd buy a silk scarf,
which feels like cool water when I touch it, even though I'd
never ever wear it.

Sara buys a bar of lavender soap for her mother and a book for
her little sister, then she tries on three pairs of jeans and six
shirts, and she keeps saying, "What do you think?" and I keep
telling her she looks great, because she does.

"When I'm a famous actress," she says, "I'm not going to have
a clothing budget, like now," and I say, "Me, neither," and I'm
laughing, because it's all so *stupid,* not having money and lying

to Sara about why I don't buy stuff, pretending I'm the sort of person who comes from the sort of family that *never wants anything*. But I want the silver hoop earrings that I dangle next to Sara's ears, and the dog-decorated socks, and the green nail polish with sparkles, and the silly cat watch with paws for hands, and the designer jeans, and six different colors of lip gloss. Is there *anything* I don't want?

No, there is not. I want it all.

# I Am Telling Lies to Sara

as we sit on the school steps,
bent over our knees and book bags,
chewing on peppermint gum,
and she is saying, *Go on, go on,*

as if she believes every lie I am making up
on the spot, out of spit and stone,
saying so sincerely I start to swallow it
myself: *My father is a great writer.*

*He took a night watchman job*
*to have time for thinking about his stories,*
*which he will write only when they're clear*
*in his head and not a moment sooner.*

I am telling these lies to Sara
hoping to hold our friendship firm,
keep it from buckling and breaking,
and I'm breathing . . . breathing . . .
breathing.

# Nine Questions to the Universe

1. Why does everyone in this family have a job except me?
2. Why do I obsess about Dad's being a night watchman?
3. Why do I imagine him in the dark, pacing by a wire fence and crying?
4. Why am I crying while I'm writing this?
5. Why did I lie to Sara?
6. Am I ashamed of Dad's job?
7. Or did I lie to Sara because I'm jealous of her family?
8. Or did I lie to Sara because I'm jealous *and* ashamed?
9. Will I ever be a better person?

# Mr. Rose and I Go Nine Rounds

1. Hi, Mr. Rose. Having a nice walk?

   What do you want? When I walk, I don't talk.

2. I just came to say hello to you.

   Hello, then! And Mr. Marty says hello, too.

3. Hey, Mr. Marty, you old dog, how are you today?

   What's that? *Old*, you say?

4. Mr. Rose, he needs a longer walk every day.

   Huh! You think you got a better way?

5. Uh-huh, sorry, but I do. He could sniff at stuff, see more of the world.

   What you got up your sleeve, girl?

6. He could use the exercise, Mr. Rose. Really, he's too fat.

   Bold, ain't you? Talking so free like that.

7. Excuse me, but more walks would be really healthy for Mr. Marty.

   Healthy? Now you're talking smart.

8. I'd be glad to do it. I'd work every day.

   Work? You're a sly one, asking for pay.

9. I won't charge much, Mr. Rose, and I promise I'll be the best.

   I'll think on it, girlie. I might say yes.

# If We Were Dogs

and we lived on Dog World, Mom would be a worried-looking Saint Bernard rescuing everyone, Spencer would be a lean, long-legged greyhound, Thom would be one of those clever no-name black dogs that are always romping around, I'd be a mutt with her nose to the ground and my best friend would be Mr. Marty, and Dad—would he be one of those sad dogs you see sometimes in the dog run, leaning against a fence, not playing like the other dogs?

# Walking with Sara after School, Talking About Race and Rice

**Vicki:** Do you mind if I ask you something, Sara?
  Do you get taken for white a lot?

**Sara:** White what?

**Vicki:** You know, a, uh, white person.

**Sara:** I don't know. Do you?

**Vicki:** Do I what?

**Sara:** Get taken for a white person?

**Vicki:** Well, um, *yes.*

**Sara:** Why?

**Vicki:** Why *what?*

**Sara:** Why are you taken for a white person?

**Vicki:** Funny girl! Because, I'm, um, *white.* Obviously.

**Sara:** Obviously? Your skin doesn't look *white* to me. I mean, paper is white and narcissus are white, and sometimes sheets are white—

**Vicki:** I never thought of it that way. My skin *is* more of a caramel color.

**Sara:** So you should be taken for a caramel.

**Vicki:** So then people would be chewing on me.

**Sara:** Watch out what you say, I'm sooo hungry. Maybe you're that caramel color—mmm, *caramels,* I love them! Turn here, let's go to Big Burger, okay?—maybe you're that caramel color because you're part African American.

*Vicki:* Hello? I don't think so.

*Sara:* You could be biracial, like me.

*Vicki:* I don't think so.

*Sara:* My dad says anyone whose family has been in this country for more than a century has a good chance of being a brother or a sister, whether they know it or not.

*Vicki:* Why does he say that?

*Sara:* My dad says a lot of things. He says human beings always want to shove other human beings into categories, boxes, pigeonholes. He says practically everyone's all mixed up, though, and I don't mean in the head. He says every group, whoever it is, thinks it's the normal one, it has the normal color, the right religion, the best country, the best way of doing things, the best language, the best food. Oh, shoot. I shouldn't have used the F word! Food, food, food. I'm famished! Oh, that Spanish rice at lunch was so good.

*Vicki:* I don't like rice.

*Sara:* Why not?

*Vicki:* What do you mean, *why not?* Because I don't.

***Sara:*** What kind of reason is that?

***Vicki:*** It's my reason. What, do you think your food tastes are the right tastes?

***Sara:*** When it comes to rice, I do. I could not live without rice. When I'm famous, I'm going to have a cook, but not just any cook. I will have a cook who knows all the rice recipes in the world. For instance, there are so many ways to make rice pudding. I have to stop this. I'm making myself too hungry! And there's Big Burger.

# Small Strawberry Shake and Large Fries for Me

Sara says, as you both stand in line in Big Burger, and she asks what you want, and you say you're not a bit hungry, adding another little lie to your life, not saying that you haven't got even the doggy bit of money needed for an order of small *small* fries, and all the time hoping your stomach doesn't growl like a dog and give you away. And at that moment, as if in a dream, your father appears in the window behind the counter. You see his profile. You see that he's wearing the green and white striped uniform. You see that he's flipping fries, and you panic and grab Sara's arm. "Let's get out of here," you say, and you can hardly breathe. "This line is way too long!" But you can't move Sara. She tells you to calm down, and she puts her arm around your waist and asks you why you're so *skitty* today.

"Skitty?" you say. "Kitty? You mean kittish or skittish?" You hardly know what you're saying. Your eyes are twitching, they're switching around, side to side, like divining rods seeking water in that underground lake that Mr. Franklin told your class about. He said it was beneath this city, and who knows, it could be right here, under this floor, and you wish it was, because your father is still there, in that window, flipping fries, and you know it's not a dream, and you want to sink to the floor, sink through it into that underground lake, plummet straight down, down deep into its watery heart. And you think how Lenny Blakely shouted, *Gotta be a fake, that lake story,* when Mr. Franklin amazed everyone with it. *You're putting us on, man! How can something be there that nobody can see?* But what you want to know is how can *someone* be there that nobody should be seeing?

You have to get away from here, away from your father in that window flipping fries. Your father wearing that green and white striped Big Burger cap, like just another kid employee, and you rush toward the door and outside. You stumble to a table and sink down, your head on folded arms. "He's working at Big Burger." You breathe out the words, almost whisper them into the cool air. And you start laughing.

Isn't it funny?

Isn't it ridiculous?

Isn't it hilarious?

Then Sara is there, munching fries from a paper cone, and she sits down across from you and asks if you're okay, and you say you're fine, you just have to go home now. And she says maybe you're getting your period, and you say, "Yeah. That's it," and you hold your stomach. "That must be why I feel so . . . you know—"

"Oh, I know!" Sara says. "I never want to eat on my first day, either. No wonder you didn't want anything."

"Yeah," you say. "No wonder."

# Mom in My Room at 8:30 P.M.

She knocks, opens the door.
*Vicki, you didn't say a word at supper.*
I'm reading, sitting on the floor.

I slide my finger into my book, look up.
*Is anything wrong? Why so gloomy?*
*Still not speaking? Still not even one word?*

What one word could I give her? *Dad?*
Then I'd have to add four more:
*—green and white stripes—*

and more
and more
and more.

# Fourteen Words from Dad
# on Saturday Morning

In the kitchen, your dad's sitting straight and still at the table, still wearing his bathrobe. He looks *gone*, as if he's waiting for something that's never going to come. "Dad, want me to make you breakfast?" you ask. "Scrambled eggs and toast sound good?"

He shakes his head and says one word. "Coffee."

You get out the machine and the filter and measure everything carefully. When the coffee has perked, you pour a cup for him and another for yourself and sit down across the table, and you can't help thinking that if he was on the father job, right now, right this moment, he'd say something *fatherly* about coffee not being good for you.

He doesn't say anything, though, not even thanks, and after a few gulps of coffee courage, you lean forward and say, "Dad? I saw you in Big Burger on Thursday."

He still doesn't say anything.

You clank down your cup. "Dad. Why are you working in that place?" Your voice sounds mean, and then even meaner when you say, "Dad! Will you answer me? Please!"

Then he says three more words. "It's a job."

"But you have a job," you say.

And now he says two more words. "Laid off."

Your stomach clenches. Didn't they like him on his night

watchman job? Is that why he was fired *again*? Your ears throb as if someone is beating drums inside them, and you know it's punishment for your mean thoughts. You want to say something good to him to make up for those thoughts, but you can't think of *anything*.

You gulp the rest of your coffee and try not to hate him for his head drooping down and his eyes almost closed, and try to believe you're not ashamed of him, but you know you are, and you're thinking you don't want anyone to ever meet him, especially not Sara.

"Dad," you force yourself to say, "can I get you anything else?" He shakes his head no, and you say, "Are you sure? You should eat something," because you know that's what your mother would say.

But he doesn't say anything. He just sits there. And you sit there. Even though you want to leave, you can't. Something is holding you.

And then he looks up and he says two more words. "Nothing helps." A wild look appears in his eyes then and seems to hurtle him out of his chair straight into the hall, but just before he disappears into the bedroom, he says six more words in such a low voice you almost don't hear them.

"I'm sorry, just so damn sorry."

## A Dream

I'm swimming in our lake,
flipping over and over, sky in my eyes,
then water, then sky, blue, blue, blue,
the loons trilling their wild ululations.
I want to follow them, fly where they fly.

## A Moment

Rain smacks against the window.
Dad is standing in my room.
He's dressed for the outdoors—
deer-hunting jacket and cap.
*Dad, it's late. Are you going—*
and then I'm asleep again,
dreaming again of loons and lakes.
Maybe I dream Dad as well.

# Poem Without a Title

*Gone for a while.*
*Don't worry.*
*I love you all.*
*I'm sorry.*

Mom found his note
on the table
under the salt
shaker.

# The First Night Your Father Is Gone

your mother sleeps
your brothers sleep
you think you will never sleep again
never, until he comes home
never, until you can stop thinking
*Why did I say those things Saturday morning?*
*Why didn't I stop him last night?*
*Why didn't I stay awake?*
*Why didn't I know?*
*Why did I go back to sleep?*

# The Second Night Your Father Is Gone

you sleep at last, then come awake hearing steps, hearing voices, your heart beating wildly. You sit up and listen, listen, listen. The house is still. There are no footsteps. There are no voices. The red numerals on the clock say 4:13 A.M. Soon, Sara's father will be on the air, his voice a real voice, the voice of a father who's left his family only to go to his job. You curl into a C and rock as if the sea were rocking you. *Sleep . . . sleep . . . sleep . . .* the sea murmurs. And, oh, you want to sleep, but sleep refuses you, and with each turn in your bed, each ache of your knees, and each creak of the floor, you see your father's face, you see his slumped shoulders, his half-shut eyes. And you can't quite hate him.

# The Third Night Your Father Is Gone

you leave your bed, dragging your quilt around your shoulders.
Windows rattle wildly. The wind is blowing. Radiators hiss, and
in the tiny room in the front of the apartment, you climb over
boxes and kneel on the cot, pushing the heat of your face against
the cool of the window, and you pray. You pray without words.
Words have left you. You kneel there, praying, praying and
waiting. Waiting for him to come home.

# Mom Tells Us a Secret

Kids, something happened once. No one knew.
It was like an ugly weed your parents
thought they could kick into dust. Now it's come
thrusting up into my face like a poison plant.
Foolish us. Thom, you're white as a fish!
All of you, just listen, okay? Please don't cry!

Your dad left me once before. Oh, I cried
then. I was only nineteen, newly
wed, a small-town girl, still fishing
for the way to live, still tied to my parents,
still not knowing how I would plant
myself in this world. Wait. Let me come

clean here. What I know now—back then, apparently
I was clueless. I never sensed anything fishy
in Larry's emotional state. True, he'd come
undone after his mom died, but he never cried.
He seemed all right. Not a seed of suspicion planted
itself in my mind. Then he left me. Left a note. I knew

I was terrified, but I turned a flat, smiling fish face
to the world. I denied my despair. No good came
of that! I was floundering. It wasn't apparent
that I was gasping for hope as if it were air, crying
if I broke a fingernail or dropped a dish. The newness
of loneliness left me exhausted. All the planning

we'd done seemed pointless. But I was also planting
flowers, telling myself *He'll be back to see the new
blooms.* I needed to dream. I was frantically fishing
for faith, but so messed up I couldn't comb
my hair or make a cup of coffee without a crisis.
Kids, telling you this might not be best for parental

status, but these past years you've seen your parents
bruised by life, and you've held up, so I think planting
the truth with you—Oh, Vicki! You're *crying.*
Sweetie, he came home that time, renewed,
so fine I hardly questioned him. For me, it came
down to trust. He'd saved himself. Why fish

for explanations? Why cry? Your parents aren't newbies
at sorrow, but I so wanted to spare you. Your dad will come
back. *He will* . . . maybe bearing gifts—plants, bread, fish.

## What They Say

Mom deplores panic: *Kids, please stay calm. You must!*
Thom says he trusts Mom, but: *I think you should call the police.*
Spencer implores: *Put up missing person signs. That, at least.*

## What I Want

For none of this to be real
to unreel this movie
to move us back
to back us out
of this mess
to miss this part of my life
to lift the curtain on a new scene
to see us together
to gather up Dad
*to know he's not dead.*

# Sara's Signature-Theory Sestina

In home base, Sara leans toward me. "V., we have to practice
writing *badly*. All famous people have awful signatures.
It proves they're important!" She smacks her forehead,
winks, but she's half serious. "We gotta write our names
big and *messy*. It's our preparation for fame,
you as a great lawyer, and me on screen and stage."

Mr. F. raps for quiet. "We're now signing up for Winslow Stage's
*A Midsummer Night's Dream*." Sara smiles. "Our first practice
writing *famously*." I nod, but Sara's game of names and fame
is not on *my* mind. "Sara," I chatter, "your signature
theory has a fatal flaw. How will fans recognize your name?"
"I'll be so famous they'll just know me." Sara tips her head.

Mr. F. gives us the *girls, please!* look, and says, "People, heads
up. Who knows the author? Dead white guy. Acted on stage.
Mega genius. Wrote plays, sonnets—anyone know his name?"
"Shakespeare?" Klaera Leesum pipes. Mr. F. smiles. "Bingo! Practice
speaking up, Klaera, okay? Now, how about the man's signature
play? Anyone?" "*Romeo and Juliet?*" Sara says. "Nope, his fame

rests on *Hamlet,* a tragedy. *Midsummer Night* has its own fame.
A girl-chases-boy-who-chases-girl-who-chases-boy saga! Your heads

around that one? Keep the sign-up sheet going, I want *every* signature on it. This is a major treat. *Live* theater. Real actors on a real stage, and it's *cheap*. Can't beat that! Plus a chance for you all to practice being adults. When did Shakespeare live?" Steve Shane, his name

synonymous with sloth and slouch, speaks up. "His first name was Will, born April 24, and the dude had sixteenth-century fame." Steve smirks. "Will and me share a birthday. I don't need practice to remember that, but he's still *boring*." Mr. F. shakes his head. "No, no, no! You're going to like this play, I guarantee. So no staging silly protests." The sign-up sheet comes closer. I can't put my signature

on it! I can't ask Mom for money, *especially* now. But a signature is required, according to Mr. Franklin. I want to fake a name! Sara's signing now with a flourish, as if she's already a huge stage star. She's a great person, but this thing about being famous sort of wears me out. Wish I could tell her what's really in my head. When she hands me the sheet, I take a deep, long breath, practicing

being calm. Messily, I scrawl my name. "*Yes!*" Sara says. "Fame's gotta come your way. Can't waste *that* signature." She taps my head. "Way better than mine. How'd you stage that? I need practice!"

# A Dozen Facts

1. Dad left us three weeks ago.
2. We need money to pay bills.
3. Mom has a plan.
4. The plan is to rent a room.
5. The room is my room.
6. The plan is to move me into the little front room.
7. That is the room we use for storage.
8. I hate this—that *is* another fact.
9. Landlady Mrs. Dann has okayed the plan.
10. Mom already has the renter.
11. Ladine Law, who works with Mom, will move in next week.
12. I hate this, and it doesn't matter.

# I Was Home Alone

when the phone rang, and it was Uncle Jud in Chicago, the
problem uncle, the drinking uncle, the can't-hold-a-job uncle,
the never-did-as-good-as-his-older-brother-our-dad uncle,
saying Dad was with him, he was okay, we weren't to worry, that
was the message, and when I tried to ask, *Does he miss us, how
long is he going to stay, doesn't he want to talk to me, is he really
okay?* Uncle Jud said, *You know what, honey, you gotta leave the
guy alone, sorry I can't talk anymore now, my phone card is running
low, just wanted you all to know things are shaping up—or down,
depending on your point of view—*and he laughed and hung up.

Later, Spencer yelled at me, *Why didn't you get the phone number?*
and my teeth started to hurt and I wanted to cry and I thought
how stupid I was and how much I hated everyone in my family,
and then Thom yelled at Spencer to quit being mean to me, and
then he came into my room and told me not to feel bad, that I
did all right, but when Mom got home and heard about the call,
she collapsed into a chair and her arms just hung over the sides
like she couldn't move, and only after a long while did she get
up and wipe her eyes and say, *Well, Jud never has a phone of his
own, anyway.*

# What Mom and I Did Friday Night:
## A List Poem

Surveyed the tiny room and counted the stacked boxes: Ten.

Emptied all the stuff in the extra bureau into suitcases.

Sat on the suitcases to close them.

Carried ten boxes and two suitcases out of the tiny room.

Shoved and pushed them all under Mom's bed.

Laughed when Mom said, "Not even room for a straw under there!"

Swept the tiny floor of the tiny room.

Put fresh flowered sheets on the cot.

Hammered hooks into the wall of the tiny room.

Taped photos on the door.

Hung a curtain on the window.

Put together a clothes rack, which refused to remain rigid.

Carried in armfuls of jeans, skirts, shirts, and socks.

Lined up shoes, sneakers, and sandals under the cot.

Declared ourselves done, finished, satisfied.

Surveyed the tiny room once more.

Closed the door.

# Message

Mom said
the flowered quilt
left on my bed would give
a nice message: *Welcome, Ladine.*
I said
I did
not want to give
any message. No, none.
Mom slapped me and cried. I was
dry-eyed.

# Ladine Law Arrives

**She** parked *her* yellow car in front of the house Saturday morning, took *her* long skinny self, which was wrapped in a long yellow coat, out from behind the wheel, reached into the back seat and pulled out a yellow suitcase, a lamp, fortunately not yellow, a cardboard box tied with, yes, yellow string, and a lumpy laundry bag—regulation white—that looked like a not-so-distant cousin to my true love, Mr. Marty, by which I mean no disrespect for that mutt, who, along with his owner, still doesn't get that I adore him.

**Then,** leaving everything on the sidewalk, *she* rang the bell, by which time I was downstairs opening the front door, and behind me were my brothers ready to carry up *her* suitcase, lamp, cardboard box, and lumpy laundry bag, and behind them was Mom, her hands out, saying in her best company voice, "Well, here you are! Welcome, Ladine." *She* and Mom kissed on the cheek. "I am a little early, I know," *she* said, with a big toothy smile, "but I was so eager, Liz, to settle into my lovely new digs that I just couldn't wait."

**Next,** we all followed Mom up the stairs, listening to Ladine. "Oh, my, those are rather steep stairs, but not to worry, Liz! I have very good balance. And this lovely girl who came down to greet me is your Vicki that you're so proud of. Vicki! Your mother's a wonderful, wonderful woman, who told me her children were all, and I quote, great kids, and that I need not be worried about noise or my privacy when abiding here among you, which is such a relief to me, as even a young girl like you can understand, I'm sure."

*After that,* she had to take a breath. I darted around *her* and opened the door at the top of the stairs. My room—excuse me, my ex-room—is right there, in front, when you enter the apartment. "Oh, my, how lovely," *she* said, walking in, standing on my rug, touching my quilt, sitting down on my bed . . . showing *her* teeth in another smile.

## Sunday Supper

"Lay-deen is the correct way
to pronounce my name,"
she instructs us as soon as
she sits down. She loads her plate,
spooning hunks of jam onto bread,
forking away my appetite.

"*Lay* to rhyme with *play*, not *la*
to rhyme with my *pa*."
She laughs and says it five, six,
seven times. "I'm forty-nine:
That's my age. I know I don't look
that old!" A horsey smile. Her teeth.

## Room Poem 1

One window.
One cot.
One clothes rack.
One bureau.
One folding chair.
One person.
Me.

## Room Poem 2

Earrings, belts, and beads hang on hooks
Jeans, sweaters, and shirts jam on hangers
I stand on the cot
touch each wall
turn, turn, turn
turn
    turn
turn

## Ladine Poem

her round black eyes
are like the olives
she piles on her plate
at the supper table.

## Room Poem Cinquain

night, dark.
the tiny room
wraps its arms about me,
holds me close. streetlight sparkles in
my eyes.

# Play Money

There are a few people who still haven't turned in
their money for the play, Mr. Franklin says on Monday.

The play is on Friday. If you have any problems, come
and see me, okay? Mr. Franklin reminds us on Monday.

People who haven't paid up, we'll work something out.
There's always a way, Mr. Franklin says on Tuesday.

I'm dead serious about this—somehow or other, you all
are going to see that play, Mr. Franklin adds on Tuesday.

Either you come talk to me or you show up with the money.
That's all I have to say, Mr. Franklin snaps on Wednesday.

# What Happened Thursday Morning

*1.* Eating doughnuts and swigging coffee, my brothers left for
school, pounding down the stairs, shouting to each other about
sports and girls. Mom in her plaid jacket and long Ladine, in her
yellow coat, big teeth munching a doughnut, went out together,
talking about carpooling. From my window I watched them on
the sidewalk. Mom threw me a last-minute, swift kiss. I danced
my fingers at her and turned away, wishing I could turn away from
knowing it was the day I had to turn in the money for the play.

*2.* Excuses tumbled uselessly through my head. I kept changing
my clothes. I couldn't decide what to wear. Plain blue shirt?
Red V-necked shirt? Pink and purple striped shirt? Red socks or
blue? Pants with one pocket or two? My clock with the yellow
and red neon hands was tick-tick-ticking, saying late-late-late,
but I still kept changing shirts, shoes, and socks.

*3.* I dreaded the moment when I would have to walk out
the door down the street, past Kravinski's Shoe Repair, Due
Brothers Bakery, the motorcycle shop, and onto Carbon Street,
past the empty factory with cracked windows and its smell of
burned paper, past all the cute little faded pastel houses and up
Fillmore Hill with the really nice big houses with lawns, which

always make me think of Sweet Road—which seems *so far away,
so long ago*—and then across the four lanes of roaring cars on
Rousebreaker Road and, finally, into school late, reporting
to the office and telling more lies. Or are they fibs?

4. I was ready to leave at last, my hand on the doorknob when I
thought, *Why am I going to school today?* If I wasn't in school, I
couldn't give Mr. Franklin the money I didn't have for the play.
But if I went to school, knowing Mr. Franklin, when he asked
for the money and I didn't have it, he'd just suck his teeth and
tell me to bring it in tomorrow, and if I didn't bring it in then,
he'd tell me to bring it in on Monday. That's the way he was.
Helpful. I didn't want his help. I didn't want him, or anyone, to
know about Dad . . . Ladine . . . money . . . *us.*

5. I stood there, thinking about this and looking into my old room,
at the curtains and the rug and the bed neatly made up, and it
seemed as if my room remembered me. As if it was inviting me
in, speaking to me. *Hey, it's your room, not hers, she's just a squatter.
You can come in. You can walk around, look around, touch things.
Make yourself at home. She's not here now. Sit on the bed. Go on, mess
it up a little. Hey, what's that on the bureau? Take a look.*

*6*. Did I know what I was going to do?

No.

No, no, no.

# What Happened Next

*1.* The purse was dark blue with a gold clasp. I picked it up and snapped it open. It smelled of powder and chocolate. I would have liked a chocolate just then. I put my hand in and what it came out with was a bunch of money. I stood there for a moment. It was like my luck had turned around completely. Then I shoved the money in my pocket.

*2.* I was calm. I went out the door and down the stairs. I was aware of being calm and thinking how Mom always wanted us to be calm. Mrs. Dann was in the hall, sweeping. I said hello, as if it was any morning. She told me I looked nice, that I had good color in my face. I said thank you. I saw Mr. Rose and Mr. Marty outside on their driveway walk. I said hello to Mr. Marty. Mr. Rose said he was still thinking about my having a job walking Mr. Marty. He called me girlie, and his mouth went up. A smile. I said, "Thank you, Mr. Rose, that's good."

*3.* I ran all the way to school, determined not to be late. I hadn't been late one single day so far. I was calm. I wasn't thinking about the money in my pocket. It was there, I knew that, but it was like a story I was telling myself. All of a sudden, I had money. I wondered how the story was going to turn out and how much money I had, but I didn't look. Looking seemed like cheating, like skipping the middle part of the story.

*4.* I walked into home base, my head hurting from running, from pounding the pavement, but only two minutes late. Mr. Franklin waved me into my seat. Sara wriggled her hand at me. "You made it," she said, as I sat down. "Just!" I touched the money in my pocket. What if there wasn't enough to pay for the play? Or what if it was a lot, like three hundred dollars— or three thousand? Stupid thought. Nobody would leave thousands of dollars lying around. "Sara." I leaned over to her. "Stupid thoughts are like spaghetti. Before it's cooked, it looks strong and straight, but you can break it into pieces. After it's cooked, it's no better. It's limp." I made her laugh. Would she laugh if she knew what I'd done? Another stupid thought.

*5.* Mr. Franklin was having one of his "teaching moments." "Some of you folks still haven't turned in your money for the play. You guys are *miscreants.* Which means someone who does something wrong or bad. Got that? Root word, *creant,* comes from the Latin for *belief. Mis,* the prefix, means bad or wrong. So a *mis*creant was a bad believer, a person who had a false religion.

From that, it came around to meaning wicked or evil. And now it just means someone who's not 100 percent good."

Sara whispered, "He could be a movie star, like Denzel Washington, don't you think? Except he's much shorter." She kept looking at me. "Do you feel okay?"

"Headache."

"Bad one?"

I nodded.

"So now when you use words like *misplace, mistrust,* or *mistake,*" Mr. F. was saying, "you know you've got a prefix going."

Was *miserable* another one? Maybe *erable* meant happy. Today I had money. I should feel *erable.*

"Okay, we're backing up," Mr. F. said. "Someone give me a definition of prefix."

Klaera raised her hand. "Means something that comes before something else," she said in her tiny voice.

*Right.* If Dad had come back before Ladine moved into our house, I wouldn't have gone in her room. That would have been a definite prefix. Everything fixed. Now everything was unfixed.

*Unfixed.* The word repeated in my mind over and over. *Unfixed. Unfixed. Unfixed.* And as the first bell rang, the calmness that had covered me like an ice cap cracked.

# Four Fives

## 1. Five Useless Facts

It's drizzling while I'm sitting on the steps outside school writing this.

I gave seven dollars to Mr. Franklin.

I had fifty-four dollars in my pocket.

Tomorrow is the play.

My chest aches, my head hurts, and my butt is getting soaked.

## 2. Five Scary Questions

Will Ladine miss the money?

Does she know how much she had in her purse?

If she knows it's missing, will she think of me first?

Will she tell Mom that money is missing?

Will she accuse me?

## 3. Five Frantic Thoughts

Maybe Ladine won't be sure how much she had.

But maybe she will be sure. *Positive.*

If she accuses me, I'll deny everything.

I won't let her look in my pockets.

I have to get rid of the rest of the money.

## 4. Five More Frantic Thoughts

I'll give the rest of the money to Mom, tell her I found it.

No, can't just hand it to her. She'll ask where I found it.

I'll say in the street on the way to school. I'll name a street, say I want her to have it. *Don't thank me, I don't need it, I don't want any of it.*

She won't believe me. She'll look at me and know I'm lying.

Even if she did believe me, she would probably boast to Ladine what a *good kid* I am, how I found all this money and shared it with her. No, not even shared, just gave it to her.

# What I Did

I got up and walked downtown. I walked fast. I knew what I was going to do. Near city hall, I found the first one—a man sitting on the street with a cardboard sign that said in scrawly black letters HOMELESS, PLEASE HELP. A small cardboard box was on the sidewalk next to him. I walked up to him and dropped some bills in the box. He looked in the box. He looked at me. "God bless you," he said. "God bless you, God bless you!"

Around the corner, a woman was standing near a restaurant. She wore a kerchief tied under her chin and a brown jacket with the lining coming out. "I need something to eat," she was saying to everyone who passed. You could hardly hear her, though. "I need something to eat. Can you give me some money?" She held out her hand and looked right at me. "Yes," I said. I was dizzy. I swayed as I dug in my pocket again. I gave her the rest of the money. Her palm was hard and bumpy and dirty. Her hand closed over the money.

# A Fight

At lunch, Sara was talking about the play. "My father saw it in New York City." She started listing all the things he had told her to watch for, and how he thought Shakespeare was so great and not all that hard to understand.

I picked at the macaroni in front of me—the same thing we'd had for supper last night. Ladine had eaten with us again. Sitting across from her—listening to her talk, watching her mouth open in a laugh at something Spencer said—I'd started feeling nauseous. I kept seeing her purse on the bureau, my hand dipping into it. . . .

I couldn't stop thinking about it at lunch, and it got all mixed up in my mind with the homeless woman, the way she snatched the money, how she had looked at me, so gratefully, as if I'd done something wonderful.

"And he says that this is just a great play to see for your first Shakespeare experience, and the thing to remember—"

"Are you still talking about your father?" I burst out. My head was pounding. "Will you please, at least, talk more quietly, *please!*"

"Excuse me? What did you say?"

"I don't want to hear anything else about the play, Sara. In one half hour, we'll get on the bus, and one half hour after that we'll be in the theater, and—"

"I know that, Vicki. What is your problem?"

"What is yours, Sara? Can't you ever talk about *anything* except your father?"

Sara stood up. "I'm going to go sit with Nikkee Garcia. Do you want to come?"

"You don't want me to come, do you?" I said.

"It's up to you. I'm not telling you what to do." She buttoned her sweater and walked over to Nikkee's table. Nikkee snapped her gum, and Sara laughed as she sat down.

I sat there, watching them talking, as if *they* were best friends. I stood up and stumbled out of the lunchroom.

On the bus, I sat with tiny-voiced Klaera Leesum. Sara was up front, in the seat behind Nikkee, playing with Nikkee's long, thick black hair. My head hurt, and I was glad that Klaera had such a soft voice. "Don't listen to Mr. F.," I said. "I mean, about your voice. It's perfect."

"How come you and Sara aren't sitting together?"

"Fight," I said.

"Serious one?"

I stared at the back of Sara's head. "Dumb one," I said. "My fault."

"Oh, you'll make up." Klaera patted my knee, as if she was my mother or something. "You'll make up," she said again.

In the parking lot, Mr. F. had us all wait while he reminded us of our manners. Then he led the way to the theater. I was with Klaera, behind Sara. Klaera gave me a look and mouthed, *Go on.*

I touched Sara on the shoulder. "Are you still mad?" Sara shrugged. "I'm sorry," I said. "I acted stupid. I didn't feel good. Like, right now, I have a pretty horrible headache."

"Really?" Sara turned to look at me. "Is that true?"

"Yes."

She pursed her lips. "Why didn't you tell me?"

"I felt too awful to say I felt awful."

"That is so—" Sara shook her head. "So . . ."

"Stupid," I supplied.

"Right. Stupid." She looked back at Klaera. "Do you agree?"

Klaera lifted her shoulders. "Stuff happens," she piped. "That's what my mom always says."

I fell into step next to Sara. "If you're not still mad, would you please smile?"

"I'm not mad," Sara said. She tipped her head in that way she had. "I just don't feel like smiling yet. Maybe, in about three minutes."

"I'll wait," I said.

The play was good, although toward the end my eyes ached so much and my stomach was doing such strange things that I couldn't keep track of what was going on. As we were all getting back on the bus, I stumbled on the stairs. Mr. Franklin caught my arm. "Steady there. So, Vicki, I know you didn't want to come to this play. Are you glad now? Was it worth it, after all?"

"Worth it?" I repeated, remembering Ladine's money. My stomach heaved, I gagged, and threw up all over Mr. Franklin's shoes.

## Sick Poem

Chattering teeth,
burning lips, swollen eyes,
aching hips. slipping into sleep.
Mom here
bends low
to my ear. *Sleep,*
*my sweetie, it's the flu,*
*you'll be fine in a day or two.*
*Rest now.*

Mom sweet,
Mom, so tender . . .
must confess . . . *everything* . . .
gather breath . . . breathe her name . . . She's gone
like air
or wind
or the thing that
is the thing that I meant
to say . . . and I'm asleep again . . .
asleep . . .

# Vicki, Nikkee, Sara & Klaera

The day I go back to school, Sara, Nikkee, Klaera, and I saunter down the hall together at lunch break as if we've been friends forever, and take one of the little round tables, drawing our chairs in close. We are elbow to elbow as they all take turns telling me they missed me this week and I should never get sick again. Then Sara leans over and kisses me on the cheek and I almost start crying, and I'm thinking, *I'm not going to be lonely ever again.*

We trade food and talk around the table, talking about everything. Tiny Klaera is filled with talk, talk flies out from her mouth and her arms and her fingers, and her hair is almost on fire with talk. She has six sisters and one little brother and six stories about each one. Nikkee is leaning on her elbows and laughing, and Sara keeps looking at me and making funny faces, and I'm happy, I'm so happy, but all the time in some far back part of my brain, like a distant land, like some place I once visited, I see a certain picture—the picture of Ladine's room— the window, the curtains, the bed, the bureau, and then my hand in Ladine's purse.

The same picture plays over and over, never changes, like a video on pause. I tell myself *Look away*, but the picture stays and the pause is endless. The picture is there as I eat, and it's there as I talk, and it's there as I laugh, and it's there as we clear our trays, and it's there as Nikkee says, "This was so cool," and it's there as we all agree to meet again tomorrow for lunch, and it's there as I think that they all think I'm like them, just like them, but they don't know anything about me, don't know that my dad has run away from us, that my mom has a stranger living in our house, and that I am a thief who stole from that stranger.

# Ladine Stood in My Doorway Last Night, a Terza Rima

Crossing her arms, she said, "Let's have a little chat."
I sat cross-legged on the cot, eating potato chips.
"We'll get acquainted, talk about this and that."

I didn't know what to say. I licked my lips,
then buttoned my shirt right up to the collar,
and kept busy making an endless chain of paper clips.

"I hear you and Thom are both quite the scholars."
I gave her a smile, but my legs and arms were weak.
She talked on and on, but she never mentioned dollars.

I kept waiting for her to yell at me, to tell me to speak,
to tell her the truth, the whole truth—some such thing.
By the time she left, I was a mess. Totally freaked.

My mind was a jittery jumble of words and sounds: *bling . . .*
*blang . . . ping . . . pang . . .* I was completely unhinged,
ready to fly out the window, just take off, take wing!

I think she knows, and like a mean drunk on a binge
she was playing with me, teasing me, taunting me.
She left me all done in—cooked, charred, *singed*.

# Words on My Mind and Where They Lead

Money

    many mercenary murmur *murder*

Bad

    bed led fed filed failed foiled *soiled*

Play

    pay price slice sluice juice just *justice*

Will

    chill cold sold seldom sailed soiled *boiled*

Did

    Dad done son sun moon man plan pin *sin*

# i can't stop thinking of these
## six absolute worst things

1. ladine knows everything and is waiting to accuse me.
2. softhearted spencer will be utterly forlorn.
3. mom will fly into a rage and refuse me her love.
4. thom will be sure i need help and he'll just hover!
5. sara will know, too, and show me nothing but scorn.
6. but the absolute worst, the most painful thought i have and what i should have put first: if dad finds out he'll blame himself and never recover.

# Dear Ms. Law

I'm writing this letter to tell you something. You won't like me when you know what I did, but maybe you already know? I guess I don't expect you to understand, but I wish you would try. I needed money for the play, and I didn't want pity. So that was the first part. The next part is this—you left your door open. You left money easy to find. I know you could say that's an excuse, and maybe it is, but I've never done anything like this before. I wasn't thinking about *after*, but if I had, I guess I thought it would be over, you know, *done*. And, for sure, if you didn't find out, that would be the end of it.

You haven't said anything, but you've been looking at me, watching me. Do you know? Are you suspicious? I had a dream that I think was about you. It was one of those sort of dark dreams, where everything is in shadow, and I was running down a street and someone was chasing me. It was you. I woke up sort of gasping, and that's when I thought about writing this letter. But now I think I won't give it to you. What if you don't know? Why should I tell you? And what about Mom? I don't want her to know, *ever*. Okay, right, I should have thought about that before I took your money, but I didn't plan to do it. That's the truth. It was an impulse. It just *happened*. Almost like it was a dream. I'm not a dishonest person. I'm not a thief. I should have put back the rest of the money. I don't know why I gave it away. I was sick, maybe that's why. I couldn't think straight. But I'm going to pay you back. That's a promise. To you, and to me.

Vicki

# Looking for Work

*1.* I like the name, so I go into The Yakkity Place first. A stubble-bearded man slouches behind a counter loaded with phones—red phones, green phones, silver phones, big phones, little phones, Mickey Mouse phones, even a hound-dog phone. "Yeah?" he says through a cloud of cigar smoke when I ask if he wants to hire me to do . . . whatever. "Naah," he says around the cigar, "repairing phones is a one-man operation, which is me."

*2.* I try every store I pass. I get a sweet "No way, sorry, honey" from Mr. Ancion in Ancion's Hardware, and a big smirk plus a finger pointed back at the door from the guy in the Jazz Coffee Shop, but what almost makes me despair is the tall woman with the big hair in Millmark's Variety who brushes me off with "Go home and drink your milk, doll," and it's all downhill from there.

*3.* I decide to try closer to home. Mrs. Dann says, "Oh, no, no, no," and tells me she's used to doing her own work. "That's what's kept me going all these years. What would I do, otherwise, sit around and watch TV? It's very nice that you're looking for work, but you'll have to try someone else. Well, now, don't look at me like that. No need to get discouraged."

*4*. But I am discouraged, so I write an *if* poem

    If pigs couldn't wallow in mud

    and books had no words

    and cats no whiskers

    and wind no whoosh

    and we had to wash without water,

    wouldn't that be discouraging?

*5*. Yesterday, after school, I saw Mr. Rose and Mr. Marty walking the driveway, both wearing short plaid coats. I went up to Mr. Rose and reminded him that I'd asked for work walking Mr. Marty. "And you never said yes or no. I think it's *yes*," I said. "So would you like to hire me right now?"

He tipped his head back and forth, then said in his growly voice, "I'll try you out. See if you're a good worker." He looked at his watch and told me to sweep the outside back staircase. I ran up to his third-floor porch, found the broom, and started sweeping. Down the steps I went as fast as I could, sweeping, sweeeeping, sweeeeeping.

When I swept the last step, Mr. Rose looked at his watch, grunted, and handed me some money. "Five pounds of dog food," he said. I didn't waste time asking what brand or if this was part of the tryout, just took off running and ran all the way to the

Hughes Super Mart. Fifteen minutes later, I climbed those three flights of stairs again, not running up them this time. I was panting, my heart knocking against my ribs. "Mr. Rose," I called, knocking on his door. He must have been waiting for me right behind the door. It opened immediately. I handed him the dog food. He gave me a nod, an almost smile, and three dollars.

Fifty-eight to go.

## Work Record 1

Swept and got dog food for Mr. Rose—$3.00
Vacuumed Mr. Rose's apartment—$2.00
Went to the store again for Mr. Rose—$2.00

## The Best

things in my life:
Mr. Marty loves me
Mr. Rose knows he can trust me
always.

## Work Record 2

Mrs. Dann has a cold. I shoveled the sidewalk in front of the
house after the big snowfall—$4.00
Took Mr. Marty for his first walk—$2.00 (It was fun!)

# In Ladine's Room

The apartment was quiet, nearly dark. My brothers were out. Mom was in bed, and Ladine in the shower. Her door was half open. I slipped in and dropped fifteen dollars on the bureau. My first payment. I arranged the bills, crumpled them a little so they would look as if they belonged there, as if she had left them there. Then I went out, but the moment I was in the hall it struck me that the money, instead of looking casually crumpled, looked planted.

She would know where it came from, who did it. If she had any suspicions, she'd just put two and two together and come up with my name. At the other end of the hall, I heard the bathroom door click open. I rushed back into the room, grabbed the bills, and looked around for a place to leave them. Under the bed? No! On the windowsill? Maybe. I heard her slippers slapping on the hall floor. I spun around, looking for a place, and then she walked in.

"Vicki?" she said. Her face was bare and shiny, her hair wrapped in a towel. "What are you doing in my room?" She almost sounded friendly, but I couldn't speak. She said it again, a little sharper. "What are you doing in my room?"

I don't remember doing this, but I must have tried to give her the money, because the next thing I knew, she was pushing my hand away, saying, "What is this? What? What's going on here?"

I licked my lips. "It's yours. Your money."

"What do you mean it's mine?" she said.

"I mean—I—I owe it to you." These words came out sort of choked, but also in a rush. "Could you just take it, please. Please just take it."

"You don't owe me anything," she said. "That's ridiculous. What are you talking about?"

"I do owe you. Would you just take it!"

"No, I won't just take it." She tied her bathrobe tighter. "Why should I take it? Tell me what this is all about."

"I owe it to you." She stared at me. I licked my lips. "I owe it to you because—I—st—" I didn't want to say that word. "I took it from you," I said. "I, uh, borrowed it."

"What?" She was looking at me with those little black eyes. "When did you do that? I don't remember that."

I swayed on my feet. Her voice was loud. I was afraid she'd wake up Mom. I tried to smile. I don't know why I tried to smile. What I really wanted to do at that moment was fall down and go to sleep and not be in her room and not be having this conversation and not have to think about what to do next. I tried to give her the money again.

"Stop that," she ordered.

"It's yours," I said. "I took money from your purse." That was it. I had said it. *Done,* I thought, and I breathed as if I had been holding my breath for days, weeks, months. *It's over.*

I was wrong. It was just beginning. I had to say again that I took money from her purse. The purse she had left on the bureau. I had to say how much I took and why I did it and when I did it. And I had to say what I did with it.

"Gave it away," she repeated. She yanked open her middle bureau drawer and took out the purse with the gold clasp. She opened it and looked inside. She took out a wad of bills and counted them. Her cheeks were blotched with red streaks.

"You gave away my money," she said. She was breathing hard.

"I'm sorry. I'm really sorry. It was a big mistake." I told her how I was working to pay the money back. I said I would pay it all, every bit of it.

"You stole from me. I worked for that money. I didn't steal it! Don't tell me you're sorry." She wrapped her arms around herself, as if she was a prize and she was afraid I was going to steal her, too. "Shame! Shame!" Her voice went higher and louder. She was going to wake up Mom. I wanted to shut the door. I wanted Ladine to shut up. I wanted to shut her up.

"Please—I told you—I'm sorry—it was an accident—I mean, I didn't plan—"

"Accident?" Her neck was red. "I trusted this family. What a fool I was."

"It's not my family's fault." I tried to whisper. "It's me. I did it."

"I trusted you all. That was my mistake. Oh, you took me in with your cute little face, your voice. Do you know that I worked a whole day to earn that money? Does that mean anything to you, Miss Thief?"

"I'll return it all, I promise."

"Promise? Why should I believe that? You're a little sneak. People like you grow up to do even worse."

My head burned as if I still had a fever. "I never did anything like this before. Honestly."

Why did I say that word? She jumped on it. She pounced on it. "Honestly?" She stepped closer. She breathed in my face. Her hands went up. I thought she was going to hit me. "You act so nice, but underneath you're nothing but a sneaky, dishonest person."

I stood there, swaying. Her breath smelled fishy. I was getting nauseous. "Are you going to tell my mom?"

She stretched herself taller, stepped back, folded her arms, and stared at me before answering. "I don't know. I have to think about it."

"Please—please don't."

"You don't tell me anything. Get out of here now. Go on. Go."

So I did.

## three days

since she caught me in her bedroom
since she refused the money
since she's spoken to me
since I begged *please don't tell.*

## three nights

she's appeared at my door
she's stood silently
she's crossed her arms
she's watched and made her plan.

## waiting

for her to tell
—or not tell.

## a dream

my little room
cracking, splitting
like pavement
after winter storms.

## Taking Mr. Marty for His Walk

Like a king, he sniffs
every tree, kid, cat, and dog
on his royal route.

## In Her Room

I leave ten dollars
on her pillow, but no note.
She will know it's me.

## At the Dinner Table

Seated next to her,
no words, but my eyes begging
Please don't tell . . . please don't . . .

## Her

eyes always watching,
ears always turned, listening.
laugh always so loud.

# Missing Dad, and Half a Dozen Other Things

1. I want to hear Dad's voice again. I want to talk to him. I want to tell him, "I miss you. Come home. When are you coming home?" Every day after school, first thing, I check the answering machine. Every day I think that this time there'll be a message from him.

2. I walk Mr. Marty in the morning before school. I told Mr. Rose no money anymore for walking him. He is the best part of my life right now.

3. Why can't Sara reach into my mind and see my thoughts? Why can't she just know what I did, so I could *stop* thinking about telling her—and then thinking, *no no no.* Yesterday, when we were talking in the auditorium, just before assembly, the words were right there on my tongue, like rafts ready to take the plunge and go over the waterfall.

4. That is my impulsive self trying to take charge of me *again.* I know it is. I know the feeling. I just want to *do it.* And I'm really afraid that one of these times, I will. I'll tell her. And then?

5. Then Nikkee would be her best friend. Ever since Nikkee came to school wearing a six-pointed Star of David on a chain, Sara thinks she is brave and *honest.* Because, she says, "Being Jewish is not so popular here, but Nikkee is right out there with it."

6. Ladine is still watching me. I know she's planning something.

7. To keep myself from going crazy thinking about her, I wrote a villanelle, which I've never done, and even though I was writing about *her,* it calmed me down.

# Vexing Myself with a Villanelle

I know Ladine is watching me.
What is she waiting for? Is she biding her time?
*Quiet,* I tell myself, *what will be, will be.*

I dream of wooing Ladine, bringing her tea,
cake, cookies, chocolate, slices of lime.
I know she's watching me.

I dream of shrinking her, turning her tiny, wee,
so small, smaller than a bug, smaller than a dime.
*Stop,* I tell myself, *what will be, will be.*

How her mind works is such a mystery.
Does she despise me for my crime?
I know, I know—I *know* she's watching me.

I think of Mom and all I want to do is flee.
Scared she'll look at me and say, *You're no child of mine!*
But again I tell myself, *What will be, will be.*

And now I write, bent low over my knees,
wishing for that time when all was fine.
I know Ladine is watching me.
I tell myself, *Stay calm. What will be, will be.*

# Eight Questions to the Universe

1. Why did I do it?
2. I mean, I know why I did it, but *why* did I do it?
3. What was I thinking when I did it? (Answer—*nothing.*)
4. Why was I thinking of nothing?
5. Is that going to be my life, always doing stupid, impulsive things?
6. What if Mr. Rose finds out?
7. What if he wouldn't trust me anymore with Mr. Marty?
8. What if no one trusts me ever again?

# Nikkee Wasn't in School Today

Klaera said, "Her mom is Jewish, you know."
Sara and I, in unison, chorused, "So?"
"So it's the holidays for them.
When you tell your sins and start fresh,
something like when I go to confession,
only they do it once a year,
and I do it once a month."
"I bet you have lots of sins," teased Sara.
"I do, yes," said serious Klaera.
"I'm doing wrong things all the time."
I leaned over the table—pleased
to hear someone else's crimes.
I want company in this strange place
of bad deeds that I've landed in.
"I have nasty thoughts." Klaera blushed.
Sara screeched, "Silly girl!"
I sank back in my seat.

# And We All Laughed at His Joke

In language arts, Mr. Franklin told us we were each going to write a letter to our favorite author or to the author of our favorite book, which, he said, "I assume you all have, and I said a letter, not an e-mail, and I want you to remember this: An e-mail is to a letter as a puddle is to a pool. Yes, you can get wet in both, but you can only swim in a pool—or drown, now that I think of it, so watch your strokes if you get into the deep end of your pool. And remember that a letter is about *something,* a letter is like a big grocery bag that can hold all kinds of things— cans and boxes, milk and butter, whatever—and don't forget a letter is neater and spelled better than an e-mail or an IM, and, speaking of abbreviations, no abbreviations! For Pete's sake, show me your stuff, show me what you got, 'cause I know you've all got it!" Then he turned and wrote on the blackboard, "Now u no whut i meen 4 u 2 do."

# The Letter I Wrote

Dear Sara,

I can *not* write a letter to an author right now. I can *not* compose my mind to compose a letter, which would only be full of phony phony *phony* stuff, because there is one thing only on my mind and it is not a letter to someone I don't know, who lives far away and has no idea who I am, and who might even be dead, and I hope that Mr. Franklin will not flunk me on this assignment because I'm writing to you instead of an author, but if he does, what will be, will be. That is my new mantra, Sara!

I know I could talk to you instead of writing this letter, but no, I can't. I have to do it this way. It's always easier for me to write than to speak. I need advice, Sara. I think you are wise. I have that feeling about you. Please be wise! I hope I'm right. I have no one else to ask. I can't tell my mom, absolutely not— that's what this is all about. And I'm afraid to say anything to my brothers.

Sara, telling you what I'm going to tell you makes me feel as if I'm running straight into traffic on the highway. Or crossing the train tracks as a train is coming. Or jumping off a high rock into a deep lake. It feels so dangerous! My heart is going so fast right this minute, just writing this, and my stomach is all in knots.

Sara, I did something wrong. Sometimes I wish I was Nikkee or Klaera, Jewish or Catholic, so I would know how to tell, confess, be cleansed of my wrongdoing, and start over fresh. But it's not possible, anyway. The person I did the wrong thing to has found out, and even though she knows I'm sorry and I'm trying to make it right, she might still tell my mother. She won't say if she's going to or not, but I think she will. I think she plans to do it. She continually watches me in a mean and significant way.

Do you have *any advice* on how I can get this person not to tell my mother? I've begged her not to, and I've apologized, and I'm trying to make up for what I did. Is there anything else you can think of that I can do? Please think about this for me. Please give me your best advice.

*Love from V.*

# *Syllables of Steel*

Why do
I keep saying
That one word I now hate?
*I'll steel myself for the next test.*
And then
I say,
*We two will steal away, Sara.*
And more. Just as a joke
I dub her *Steel*
*Girl,* not
at all
in the moment
getting the real joke-jolt
of it. But deep down, don't I hope
she is?

# Memo to Myself

Try not to be mad at Sara.

Remember she's your best friend.

Tell yourself she thinks she's giving you good advice.

Remind yourself she doesn't know what you did, and she doesn't have to know.

Remember that you are trying to curb your impulsive side.

Ask yourself how you can still forget that.

# Saturday Afternoon

She says,
*How do I know*
*how much you really took?*
I say, *I told you. I don't lie.*
She smirks.

She's like
a box stuffed full
with hidden things. She takes
out two words, shakes them in my face.
*thief . . . liar.*

## Saturday Night

Late, dark.
They're all sleeping.
I can't sleep. I can't. Can't.
Ladine is going to tell Mom.
I know.
She will.
I saw her eyes.
She's going to do it.
She's just waiting for the right time.
She'll tell.

## Later. 3:30 A.M.

I tiptoed into Mom's room. She was still, all curled up. I bent over
her and listened to her breathing. I whispered, "Mom, I have to
tell you something." I knelt and leaned my head on the bed next
to hers. "Mom," I whispered, "I stole money. I stole from Ladine.
I'm sorry, Mom. I'm paying it back. Please don't hate me." She
went on sleeping. Her breathing was peaceful, as if she heard me,
and it was okay, she understood and forgave me. I tiptoed out.
Now I can sleep. I'm so tired, but I said it. I did it. I told her. I
know it wasn't the real thing. It was like a rehearsal. Tomorrow
I'll really tell her. I'll do it tomorrow morning. I promise myself.

## Sunday Late Morning

I overslept.

## Sunday, Noon

As soon as I walk into the kitchen,
Mom asks, "Is it true you stole from Ladine?"
I take a breath, meaning to explain, but
instead I blurt, "She told you? I'm screwed!"
Mom gasps and knocks over her coffee cup.
"So now my daughter is not just a thief."
Her mouth has turned crude, rude, rough. Awful.

I plead, "I didn't plan to do that . . . thing.
It just happened, like a crash, like lightning."
"Stop!" She wipes up the coffee spill. She screams,
"Why didn't you ask me for what you need?
For good god's sake, you're not a homeless waif!"
Then she weeps. I hate her for doing that.
Her tears make me hate myself even more.

# Portrait of Mom

after she knows all:
red, blotchy, tear-streaked cheeks, tight
white lips, scary eyes.
I never saw her this way
with that ugly, angry face.

# Skidding on the Icy Path of Life

Sitting on snowy steps with Sara,
I said we should go someplace else, not so wet.
"But, Vicki, this is a perfect place to talk."
"She said desperately," I added.
(Although, after Mom, *not* in a jokey mood.)

Sara liked the joke, though. She tousled my hair
and threw me such a sweet look that *I*
threw over all sense and let myself forget
the very things I've been trying so so hard
to learn—to think, *think,* before acting.

I blurted out everything, trapped myself,
told Sara the entire sad, stupid story.
She stared hard at me. "Oh, so that's why
you wrote that letter, and what you didn't want
to tell your mother. How dumb. How very dumb!"

Before, when I imagined telling,
I knew she would hate what I did, but always
I made up a happy ending: sympathy
and understanding, Sara saying

I wasn't a bad person, just slid, slipped up,
skidded a bit on the icy path of life.

But now she was mad, calling me names.
I thought I'd lost her. I pressed my lips tight.
"Vicki, I would have lent you money," she said,
"in a heartbeat. You didn't know that?"

All I knew was that I couldn't—just couldn't—
talk about Dad or the family—nothing.
Yet now I'd done it, spilled it all out,
the whole deal—everything! I tried not to cry.

# When

Sara yelled at me
when I told her everything
when she glared at me
when we walked down the street
when I tried again to explain
when she kept saying, *I don't get it, you shouldn't have done it*
when I could barely speak
when we parted at the corner
when I walked home alone
when I went up the stairs, wanting to cry
when I went in the house and didn't cry
when even Thom looked at me as if he didn't know me
when I didn't eat supper
when I went into my room and closed the door
when I lay on my bed and pulled at my hair
when I tried to think about something else
when I wondered how to make things right
when I couldn't think of anything . . .
what should I have done? what? what?

## Last Night

even though I told Mom my debt was almost paid off, she kept asking why why *why* I took that money. It made me crazy and I shouted at her and she shouted back. And then Spencer said to Thom, "Let's get out of here. This family is nuts." He looked ready to cry, and it made me even crazier, and I shouted at him, too, "Don't you dare cry! What do you have to cry about, *mama's boy.*" Mom slapped me, the second time in my life she's done that. A moment later, she hugged me and said she was sorry, so sorry. I didn't say anything. I didn't hug her back. I felt myself passing over something, like going over a bridge. On one side, the side I'd always been on, I could cry and pout and shout, but on the other side, it was different. That's where I am now. I've crossed over that bridge—and I'm never going back.

# Story About Friendship

This morning, Sara caught up with me in the hall, just as I was ready to walk into home base. "Vicki, wait up."

"What do you want?"

"I have something to say to you. Hold on!"

"*What?*"

"Uh, this isn't easy, but I have to say it."

"*What?*"

"Um—okay, here it is. I was a jerk the other day. I talked to my mom, and she helped me see that I was way out of line. You did something wrong, yeah, but I didn't have to come down on you like that. My mom said who am I to be so righteous." She put her arm around me. "Vicki, can you forgive me?"

Just like when we first met, she stunned me. For a moment, I wanted to hurt her back, the way she hurt me. But I'm lucky sometimes. I don't always do *everything* wrong.

"Sara," I said, "I kept secrets from you. It was hard, it made me sort of crazy. I stopped thinking straight. My brain was *mush*, I'm not kidding! I'm glad now that I told you that mucky story of mine, but, Sara, it was so awful thinking you hated me and I'd wrecked our friendship."

"I never hated you. I went home and cried my eyes out! V., will you promise me something? That if you ever need anything again, you'll come to me, and, at least, we'll talk things over? Like friends should."

"I promise," I said. Then we linked arms and walked into home base.

## Poem About Friendship

I was wrong
    to keep my heart
        closed tight
            as a trap.

# Just Like That

In the kitchen this morning
Dad is sitting at the table
with the newspaper and coffee.
I plunk down hard and hum
out, "When did you get back?"
"Late last night. You were sleeping."

His eyes at half-mast, he looks half asleep.
It's cold again this morning.
My hands are frozen. I push back
my chair, push away the table.
Taken by surprise, I want to hit him.
Is it that thought that sets me coughing?

The newspaper falls from the table.
Dad bends for it, groans. "It's my old back
problem," and then *he's* coughing.
I wonder if I'm still asleep,
if this is just a dream about him.
Any moment I'll wake to the real morning.

He leans over, kisses my cheek, sits back,
starts to speak, then stares into his coffee.
He's shaking. All my nasty thoughts get tabled.
Trounced. Just that swiftly, I slip-slide
away from that mix of meanness and mourning.
*Dad is really here.* I'm looking at him,

and I'm ready to sing out a praise hymn.
*My dad's come home.* Then . . . a flashback
of all the bad moments before this morning
hits me, snatches away the joy, fixes a coffin
for it. Memories whap me—stinging slaps,
one after another. Dazed, I start table

talking. Babbling something. It's all tabled
now, lost somewhere in my mind. As for him—
Dad might as well have been asleep
or still AWOL from his family . . . Back,
was he? Maybe in body. I poured coffee,
drank it. The light had drained from the morning.

I had an instant of humming joy that he was back
with us, at the table, and then—*zip*. So he's here, coffee
cup in hand. And it's just another sleepy Saturday morning.

# A Family Conference

Late Sunday afternoon, we all went into the kitchen. Mom made a pot of cocoa, shut the door, and we sat down around the table. It was sleeting outside.

"Kids," Dad said, "I just want to say I'm home now for good. I'm home now, and I'm all right."

"Where were you, and what was the matter?" Spencer said. "Mom told us—"

"Spence!" Mom said.

Dad put his hand over hers. "I was with your uncle Jud in Chicago, staying in his apartment."

"We knew that." I pushed away my cocoa cup. "He called once. You didn't."

Mom looked at me, and I shoved back my chair. "Don't you go," she said.

"I wasn't going to," I said, but the truth was that I was ready to run out of there if anyone said *anything* to me about Ladine or the money, or anything at all. If they hated me so much, why was I even here?

"I asked Jud to phone," Dad said. "I wasn't ready yet to do it myself. I was sick. Nothing physical—but *sick,* anyway. My mind was sick. Do you understand?"

"Of course," I said. "I'm not a child."

Dad nodded. "I was laid low by a pretty serious depression. I guess you all knew that, it must have been pretty apparent."

"Dad," Thom said, "if you could only have talked to us—"

"I was too . . . depressed to talk." Dad held his cup, as if he was warming his hands. "And the worse I felt, the less I could talk. I'm sorry for everything you had to go through. If I could take it back, if I could undo it—but there are some things we do that we can't undo. We just have to live with them." He tipped back in his chair and closed his eyes.

"Does anybody want to say anything?" Mom asked.

"Yes," I said, "I do. Dad." I waited for him to open his eyes. "Everybody knows what I did. I guess you should know, too. I took—"

"I know," he said. "Your mother told me. She told me everything."

After that, there didn't seem to be anything else to say. Our family conference was over.

# A Family Crisis Acrostic

Like a bear with meat, Mom's hunched over, except
It's the TV screen and what's on it that she's gobbling,
Zapping her hands together, clapping for the Lady Lucks.
Maybe she wishes she was there on that team, a girl with luck,
A girl with another life, me not making her life so tough.
Reasonable, *really nice* is what we kids always said about Mom,
Not like other moms, never rough, so much kinder, better, the best.
Easy to say then. That was before *everything*. Now I can't forget
That she brought home the Law that made me an outlaw.

"Vicki," Mom says, not looking at me, just ordering.
"In the kitchen, water's boiling. Bring your dad a
Cup of tea. Me, too." Not even a please. I walk by them like a
Kid who sees nothing. That's the way it's been for a week.
I don't want to be around Dad. I don't want to see him. I'm
Mute to him. We've hardly talked all week. Mom's mad
At me now for that. *Too bad!* I pour boiling water over tea bags.
Raucous noises, snorts, and laughs rise from my brothers' room.
"Nice little sister, bring us tea, too. What are we, chopped liver?"
"Eeeuu," I shoot back. "I'm not coming in that stinky, sweaty room."
They laugh, tell me I'm cute. They know how to let go, forget.

*L*adine walks into the living room in her yellow coat.
*A*ll she wants, she says, glaring at me, is Mom's and
*D*ad's attention while she states her case—her "reason"
*I*s what she calls it: "My reason for leaving this place."
*N*o one moves while she says her piece.
*E*xactly this: "I will not stay in this house any
*L*onger. I have made up my mind. I've found
*A*nother place to live, somewhere I can feel safe.
*W*hat was done to me here was like . . . like *rape*."

"*L*ady!" My silent father springs to his feet, full of speech.
"*A*re you aware of what you're saying?
*R*ape? You're calling my daughter's mistake *rape*?
*R*ight now, I want you to take those words back.
*Y*ou can just unsay them, and we'll let it go.
*M*y daughter did wrong, but that's crazy
*A*nd I think you know it. Look, none of us should be
*R*ighteous. We've all made mistakes. We hope you stay.
*N*o, really. Liz and I have talked it over. If you can
*E*xtend some forgiveness to Vicki—she's paid you back.
*T*ake into account her age, my problems, other factors—"

"Out of the question." That was Ladine's response.

Up went her arm, as if she wanted to hit me, slap me down.

Really, in a weird way, I understood. She was as mad at me as I

Was at my father. When you're that mad, you want to strike.

Hadn't I wanted to hit him? My brothers wandered in then.

Out went Ladine, suitcase in hand, thumping down the stairs.

"Lord, lord," Mom half whispered. "What do we do now?"

"Easy come, easy go." A Spencer joke, but no one laughed.

Feeling nauseous, nearly faint, I sank down on the floor,

And, despite that bridge I'd crossed, I wanted to cry again.

My father had defended me! I gripped my hands tight

In my lap. "Dad," I said, "everyone. I'm sorry! Sorry. I

Let you all down. This mess—it's all my fault."

"You're not alone in this," Mom said. "Families stick together."

# An Intense Conversation with My Parents

**Vicki:** I apologized, I paid her back. Why couldn't she forgive me? I'll never make a mistake like that again.

**Dad:** Probably not, but you'll make other mistakes. Living is about learning, and making mistakes is all part of life. I'm proof of that.

**Mom:** Larry, depression is a sickness, not a mistake. And Vicki, you need to understand that Ladine doesn't have any family, and being alone is one of the hardest things in the world. She thought she'd found a place with us, and when this . . . thing . . . happened, she got scared. I'm sure that's why she couldn't forgive you.

**Dad:** If you think of yourself as a car—

**Vicki:** I've never once thought of myself as a car.

**Dad:** When I left, I was like a car without a driver, going downhill with no brakes.

**Mom:** Look, I want to say again, no matter how mad we get or how many mistakes we make—and I've done my share—we're family, and that means we don't give up on each other. Are you with me on this, Vicki?

**Vicki:** I guess so.

**Mom:** Is that the best you can do?

**Vicki:** I'm sorry if I'm not enthusiastic enough for you.

**Mom:** Oh, Vicki, please. Do you have to talk in that tone of voice?

**Vicki:** It's just my voice. It's just me.

**Mom:** Okay. Okay. I know things have been difficult. Can we somehow get back to where we were before this nasty business?

**Vicki:** Mom, where we were before is someplace I'll probably never be again.

**Mom:** That makes me sad. That really makes me sad.

**Vicki:** I'm sorry, Mom. I'm just trying to tell you the truth.

# Dad and I Go Out Together

On a wet and windy morning, a gray sky Sunday
morning, Dad and I, bundled in hats and scarves and sweaters,
trot side by side through silent streets, and what I want to say
lies tangled in my throat: *Dad, you didn't write us a single letter,*

*not even a note.* Then, in the park, circling the gray stone lions,
it comes bursting out. "It was cruel of you to leave us that way!"
Sweat beads his lip. "We all make mistakes, Vicki. None of us are giants.
I wanted to be healed, whole—and home again. That's all I can say."

All? Is that all? I wind my scarf tighter, turn . . . and turn again.
Wind picks up my hair, whispers, *Will you go on being tough and mad,*
*will you go on being sad, stubborn, and mean . . . or will you bend?*
*Let go of anger . . . let go, let go . . . this is your dad, your dad . . .*

I breathe in the words, breathe in the wind, breathe out a joyful shout,
and in that radiant instant, I know, I know this is what love is all about.

# What I Believe

I believe my parents stick together
through thick and thin, and even when I don't like them
it's good that they do. I believe my mother has become thin as a stick
and my father's belly has thickened. I believe I love my family
but sometimes I can't stand them, and they can't stand me, and then
things get sticky. I believe Dad is getting better, but he might never
be as strong as he once was, and I believe my brother Spencer
doesn't want to believe this.
I believe it's good for me to write things
because first it might hurt, but then it helps
and even though I don't know exactly why it helps
I believe it may be because the words I write
come from someplace true and deep inside me—
although not always. I believe this is the truth.
I believe it's hard to be truthful all the time
but I believe I'd better start trying harder.
I believe my parents are trying to forgive me
and my brothers still love me
even though I didn't do things right.
I believe it would be good for everyone to write
and it doesn't have to be poetry or hard work.
I believe in doing homework because I like doing it
and I believe in people doing things they like to do

as long as they don't hurt anyone doing them,
which is sometimes a lot harder than it sounds.
I believe the words *hard* and *hurt*
have occurred too often in this poem.
I believe that sometimes I think that things I write
are poetry, and they aren't, but I'm still fond of them.
I believe I'm now a best friend to Mr. Marty,
but when I take him for a walk, Mr. Rose gets potato-faced,
which I believe means he might be jealous, and this makes me laugh
although I don't know why, but I'm awfully glad of any laugh,
because I believe I've been sour as a lemon lately.
I believe in eating lemons raw, potatoes with heaps of butter,
and my toast burned, even though Mom says it's carcinogenic.
I believe it's heaven to use words like *carcinogenic*,
*catacombs, cantankerous,* and *charitable.*
I believe I'll visit the catacombs someday
and be a lawyer who helps people in trouble
and I'll live with three cats and one dog.
I believe despite my faults I'm dogged
and I will do the things I want to do
in this world, which is a belief
that makes me as happy
as writing this poem.